VIVIAN

Christina Hesselholdt, born in 1962, studied at the Danish Academy of Creative Writing in Copenhagen and published her first novel in 1991. She has since written sixteen books of prose, including several novels and short story collections, and has received numerous awards. *Vivian* won the Danish Radio Best Novel Award 2017 and was shortlisted for the Nordic Council Literature Prize in 2017. In 2018, Christina Hesseldholdt received the Grand Prize of the Danish Academy for her body of work. Her latest novel, *Virginia is for Lovers,* was published in Denmark in 2019.

Paul Russell Garrett translates from Danish and Norwegian. He serves on the management committee of the Association of Danish-English Literary Translators (DELT) and is Programme Manager for a theatre translation mentoring programme, [Foreign Affairs] Translates!

'*Vivian* is a fascinating, ingeniously constructed piece of documentary fiction. The novel's short sections illuminate Vivian Maier in brilliant flashes without ever dispelling her singular mystery.'
— Adam Foulds, author of *Dream Sequence*

'Christina Hesselholdt transposes one of the greatest enigmas of twentieth century photography, Vivian Maier, with a synaesthetic delicacy. Part eerie acapella of confessions, part hoarder's clippings come to life, Hesselholdt's exceptional work on the life of Vivian Maier is as rare and roguish as the artist herself.'
— Yelena Moskovich, author of *Virtuoso*

'Like its protagonist, this ambling story relishes the connective, startling minutiae of the commonplace encounter. ... Out of Vivian's torrent of travel, homelife, and familial resentment, Hesselholdt provides flashes of odd loveliness.'
— Zack Hatfield, *ArtForum*

'Only the second of Hesselholdt's works to be translated into English – adroitly so by Paul Russell Garrett – this fragmented, polyphonic novel plays with the enigma of its subject: "Vivian", "Viv", "Vivienne", "Miss Maier", "Kiki", "V. Smith", depending on the scene or her mood. ... Never sacrificing the opacity that makes Maier so fascinating, [*Vivian*] is as strange and mercurial as the inscrutable figure at its centre, and as prickly too. But then, as Hesselholdt has Vivian explain to one of her small charges, "Art is not somewhere you feel comfortable."'
— Lucy Scholes, *Financial Times*

'Hesselholdt brings Maier to life, luminously: looking down into the viewfinder on the top of her Rolleiflex camera, seeing the image for the first and last time.'
— Tom Overton, *frieze*

Fitzcarraldo Editions

VIVIAN

CHRISTINA HESSELHOLDT

Translated by

PAUL RUSSELL GARRETT

'Have you the Heart in your Breast– Sir
– is it set like mine – a little to the left –'
— Emily Dickinson

Narrator (that's me clattering about... when I lift the lid to see if the characters have come to the boil).

One fine day, the fourth Thursday of November 1929, before the family had been separated, the turkey had just come out of the oven and was resting on the kitchen counter. Maria, who was from the country and could make herself sound like a turkey when she wanted to, made a gobbling sound over the turkey to amuse her husband Charles and her daughter Vivian and her son Charles (also known as Carl) and perhaps also her in-laws who had arrived with Carl because he lived with them, and the ludicrousness of the turkey increased with each impression. They were immigrants and the observance of all that this festive occasion dictated, from cranberry sauce to pumpkin pie, was a way of clinging to America, for them that big turkey *was* America... That day there was a knock at the front door of the Maier household: it was Julius Hauser, the short and normally so meticulous brother of Vivian's paternal grandmother, a man who was in the habit of bringing his slippers with him in a paper bag to guard against the cold floors, but for whom things had obviously gone awry. 'Fill the tub,' Charles Maier shouted to his wife Maria Jaussaud Maier (*Jaussaud,* her French maiden name, had from the time she got married functioned as a middle name and now stood shuddering after advancing to the front ranks). 'You're not setting foot in the living room till you're clean, Hauser,' Charles said to Julius. Vivian could see that her father did not want to touch him, and searched for a clean spot on his jacket where he could take hold, but there was no clean spot, and with a look of disgust (upper lip drawn back towards the nose as his mouth stretched) he grabbed Hauser's soiled collar with two fingers (soiled with vomit and dirt from the sidwewalk, onto which he had keeled over in his drunken state, and likely spent the night – it was a miracle he was not hurt) and dragged him towards the kitchen where Vivian's mother was boiling some water. They shut the kitchen door but after a little while, Vivian eased the door handle down and pushed the door open a crack. She saw: Julius sitting in the zinc bathtub, her father scrubbing his back, her mother washing his clothes in a pot on the stove as a stray sleeve attempted a wave but was forced back down. The kitchen was steamy and smelled of boiled intestines, and Julius' face and upper body had a reddish tint. Vivian knew that he was or had been a butcher (at a hotel, maybe that just meant he was the one responsible for the meat, but she didn't think about that, she was only three years old) and that's why she didn't like him. She could have sworn that only her one eye was visible through the crack, the one eye that she forced to keep watching and watching as Julius was scrubbed in the large tub, but Julius Hauser suddenly saw that eye through the crack and shouted: 'Do come in, my little girl!', at which point her mother turned away from the stove with the dripping spoon and her father whacked Hauser over the head with the bath brush, shouting at him in German, calling him a scoundrel.

When Charles Maier struck him with the brush a second time, Hauser stood up in the tub and nearly slipped, grasping at thin air in the cramped kitchen, and precisely how it happened nobody managed to see, but the turkey fell into the tub with him. 'Do you need scrubbing too?' he shouted, and forced the large golden crown down between his legs (and here you are invited to picture the scene in that Fellini film, I can't remember what it's called, where a group of boys catch a group of chickens and then screw them or pretend to screw them, each boy with a flapping chicken pressed against the groin, and the flapping wings look like propellers that drive the boys' bodies forward), but then Charles hit him again, and he drew the turkey from the depths and handed it to Maria. She stood at the ready with a towel and accepted it like a child emerging from the waves that had to be towelled down, as all disdain gave way to solicitude, the thought of the Great Depression ever-present – it was a colossally expensive turkey.

All the same, Julius Hauser was not allowed to join them in the dining room even though he was now perfectly clean, and Vivian did not want any turkey because it had been between the butcher's legs, where she had seen some shrivelled skin dangling when he stood up in the tub, but her mother, born 11 May 1897 in the French Alps, told Vivian Dorothea Therese Maier, born 1926 in New York City, that it had been washed and that Vivian *had to* eat it, but Karl (in America, Charles) Wilhelm von Maier, born in Austria in 1892, seized the opportunity to pick a quarrel and said that she didn't have to – 'It just leaves more for us.' A little later he told Maria for the umpteenth time in their marriage that she had no clue as to what a man was, alluding here to the fact that she had never had a father, since her father, Nicolas Baille as he was called, had run off to America, where he became a herder somewhere out west, after getting Maria's sixteen-year-old mother pregnant when he was only seventeen himself. To which Maria replied: 'And in allowing my birthday to become my wedding day, I allowed one accident to grow into the other.'

The quarrel that day gave Charles Maier an excuse to drink, and as Julius Hauser was scrubbed up and sitting on a chair in the kitchen anyway, Charles enlisted him as a drinking companion. Shortly thereafter, Julius Hauser was drunk again and together they struck up old Austro-Hungarian drinking songs while the rest of the family (which besides Maria and Vivian and her older brother by six years, included Charles' parents and their daughter Alma and her husband, Josef Korsunsky from Kiev, a Manhattan silk trader and proprietor of the Colony Silk Shop, now going by the name Joseph Corsan, and Vivian's maternal grandmother, a celebrated French chef who worked at all the grand households, was also there; the guests, all immigrants, were all hard-working, even those of an advanced age) arrived during the quarrel to join them for turkey dinner – it was just as crowded in the living room as it is in this paragraph, but now the entire cast has been, if not introduced, then at least mentioned, hopefully none forgotten. And there they all sat, around the dining table, listening to their father, son, husband, brother, son-in-law, Charles Maier, getting drunker and drunker in the kitchen. His parents and Maria's mother gave one Austro-Hungarian and French sigh after the other and gesticulated mechanically, agreeing that this bold-as-a-butcher's dog Austrian and French cat should never have married. By meticulously criticizing and pillorying only their own child and never the other's, the two grandmothers managed to develop a lifelong friendship, in spite of the family's madness.

'I have no desire to ever see that drunkard again in my life,' Maria Hauser von Maier said of her son. 'He is a worthless individual.'

'My daughter is indolent and malicious,' Eugénie

Jaussaud replied.

'But Carl and Vivian...' Maria Hauser said.

'Yes, for them I would fight like a lion,' Eugénie said.

The following day Maria left Charles for the umpteenth time, leaving the name Maier behind. She left her son with the in-laws, with whom he had already lived for several years, having first done a spell at a children's home, taken out of harm's way of his parents' violent quarrels.

'They didn't want me,' he later said of his parents. 'The only thing they gave me plenty of was names.'

From an early age he was led down the path of name-bewilderment, for he was baptized not once but twice, thanks to the inability of his Catholic mother and Lutheran father to reach an agreement about anything whatsoever. First baptized Charles Maurice Maier (and into the bargain his mother entered *filius naturalis* – that is, born out of wedlock, even though he was born nine and a half months into their marriage – in the baptismal record), he was then baptized Karl William Maier. From then on the French side of the family referred to him as Charles and the Austrian side of the family as Carl, which was, to put it rather crudely, enough to make you schizophrenic, a diagnosis he did in fact receive at some point late in the 1950s, by which point he had long been calling himself 'John William Henry Jaussaud (Karl Maier),' the American, French and German captured in solidarity.

The most surprising thing about Viv's baptism (she was only baptized once) was that her mother suddenly gave herself a new middle name on the baptismal record. She called herself Justin, as though she wanted to imply that she'd had Viv with a Mister or Monsieur Justin. But if you compare brother and sister they have (in profile) the same sharp, upturned nose and slightly receding chin. There is a windswept look to them. A gust (or a hand) seems to have brushed over their features too roughly.

Maria took Vivian with her when she left. She *said* there was no room for two children in the apartment where she had taken lodgings with the portrait photographer Jeanne Bertrand on the sixth floor of 720 St Mary's Street... but it was not very far from the in-laws' home, just a short walk away through St Mary's Park.

Narrator
And now a great leap forward to 1968.

Mr Rice
On the way to the train station to pick her up, I came to think about my childhood nannies and felt a lovely sensation pass through my body of being enveloped by arms and barms, of someone who only wished the best for me bending over to pick me up and embrace me. I had not yet met Vivian Maier – Sarah had interviewed her alone. This time we wanted to be sure of making the right choice, and she had also made an awfully good impression on Sarah (despite mostly being interested in whether there was an express service from our place into town), and she had only just moved in with us (I was still away on a business trip) when her father died and she left to attend the funeral.

Narrator
The platform emptied, options disappeared, and only she remained, six feet tall and slender as a reed, just off the train from New York City, practically no luggage, and Mr Rice's sweet dreams (of a curvaceous nanny in a short, flouncy dress and possibly an apron, constantly within reach, like an incandescent lamp, better yet, an open fire in the room next to Ellen's but Ellen would be asleep or playing in the garden, and he had long arms, no matter where the nanny was in the house, his hands sprung up, up her thigh and around her buttocks, and there's an arm jolly well poking up by her neckline, wherever did that come from) faded out.

Mr Rice

I wouldn't say I had to tilt my head back to look her in the eyes, but very nearly, and after having been immersed in boyhood memories, I was confused by the fact that she was taller than me (as though I was still a little boy).

'May I offer my condolences,' I said, and went to meet her with an outstretched hand. Her height made me automatically expect a grip that left a lasting impression but her handshake was cautious and clammy. 'Vivian Maier,' she said, 'just call me Viv.' It sounded flighty, like someone who was gone before you knew it – Viv, and she was gone. She had hardly any luggage – at the time, mind you; there sure was plenty later – a valise and a purse over her shoulder, and a box camera strapped around her neck hanging at navel height, a Rolleiflex, I had always wanted one like that. We got into the car, and as we drove, we talked about what we saw. She had been working in Chicago since '56. We had replied to her ad in the *Chicago Tribune.*

Narrator

As early as the late forties she had been to Chicago to visit her brother Carl at a mental hospital. When his grandmothers died, he completely fell apart. It took him an hour to eat the apple she had brought him. He was severely debilitated by his medication. When he got up from the chair and followed Viv to the locked door, he moved in fits and starts. The only thing he said was, 'I'm so dirty.'

Mr Rice
A little way ahead lay a horse in the gutter with its head in a pool of blood; she rolled down the window and took a picture of it. I guess it had been bound for the slaughterhouse when the tailgate flew open, the horse fell out and struck the road at full tilt. Thus it had avoided the stockyards. And then it had just been left there, in the blink of an eye made uneatable, unusable. With its big dead eye staring at a pool of its own blood. A horse-drawn carriage went past, and the horse did not so much as send it a sidelong glance – admittedly it did have blinders on, but it must have been able to smell the dead horse. However, it was indifferent and remained so, a proper city horse. I remembered reading at some point that you can't get a horse to drink from a bucket that had once held blood, which was an oddly inexact piece of information, because at some point the bucket must have stopped smelling of blood.

'My first photograph in Chicago today.'

It was Sunday and there wasn't very much traffic. Every time she went to take a photograph, I slowed down or came to a complete stop. She appreciated that. She worked like lightning and was very assured. It goes without saying that to a certain extent you see your surroundings anew when you are with a newcomer and even more so with someone snapping away so eagerly. Would I have noticed the old lady standing in the middle of her narrow, short plot of land, squeezed in between apartment buildings, once a garden, now a repository for old windows and other scrap, the ground completely bare except for a couple of dying shrubs? It got me thinking about how the garden might have looked before she got so old. About how everything that you have so diligently maintained can wind up as a dumping ground, without you being able to do anything other than grab your cane and drag yourself out into the degeneration and just stand watching it decay further. Here I happened to think about Sarah and her obsession with her garden. I think she is too young to spend so much time on it. I associate gardening with a later stage of life. My mother was older when she started to parade her roses, having long since lost her own bloom. Or would I have noticed the hoarding in front of another apartment building that was constructed of nothing but doors, a fence of doors, some of them with knobs still on, so that they were invariably viewed as entrances and made the fence look like the set of a comedy, where the protagonist is always disappearing through another door just as his pursuants reappear on stage.

'The Kodak Girl,' I said to her.

Narrator

Here he was referring to the series of women and girls who had since the late nineteenth century been used to advertise Kodak, thus illustrating that Kodak cameras were so easy to use that even women could work them, and pandering to the female user of Kodak, who was depicted free as a bird in the wild, camera strapped around her neck, capturing her own version of reality, soon identifying pre-existing Kodak moments, simultaneously contributing to women's liberation from the confinement of the home and giving them the chance to roam freely in nature without the protection of a male companion, because the fact is, in the majority of the advertisements with annually alternating Kodak Girls, she is alone.

Maybe the adverts had not been sufficient, because in an article in *Popular Photography* entitled, 'Are Woman Allergic to Photography?' the following invitation can be read: 'Ladies, take yourselves out of exile and make friends with your camera! There is a world out there waiting for the eye of the camera woman.'

Mr Rice

'No, the Rolleiflex Person,' Viv replied.

'I look forward to seeing the pictures you've just taken.'

She replied that she did not always have them developed because it was too expensive.

'And besides, I have seen them,' she said, tapping the box camera, 'down here.'

'Why don't you just develop them yourself?'

And so she did, but she was not particularly keen on it. A little later she said: 'I'm only good at things that interest me.'

I hoped that she was interested in children and cooking and housekeeping.

'Children, yes,' she said.

Mrs Rice

When I've been sleeping with a man for some time (I did at least manage to have *one* other man before I got married), let's say two or three years, it starts to feel incestuous, as though I know him far too well to perform the in all respects age-old steps with him; it starts to feel wrong and awkward, and it's been like that with Peter for a long time. When I've known a man for some time, let's say two or three years, I start to have a hard time sitting at the table with him. I simply can't stand watching him eat, he seems to be chomping his food, and I can't help imagining the food in his oral cavity being pulverized into an indistinct mass, a gruel or a porridge, a grey stream that vanishes down his throat, which I'm very sorry to say is now more like a sewer to me.

Narrator
She suffers from aesthetic hypersensitivity, the poor thing.

Mrs Rice
I hide it as best I can. I try to look away when he is chewing. Why does this sickly hypersensitivity only manifest itself after I have known the man for some time? And why is it reserved for the man I share a bed and a table with? My psychologist has not been able to answer that. The table manners and chewing of other people don't bother me in the least, unless they are particularly glaring, thank goodness, otherwise I would almost be crippled, since a significant chunk of human interaction in this world revolves around consuming something together, be it food or be it drink.

Narrator
She is (still) young and full of burning desire, but Mr Rice has now become her brother and a disgusting masticator, so what does she do to let off steam? She throws herself at the soil, in the garden, she doesn't use a shovel but bores into the ground with her hands, with her fingers and nails, and with no gardening gloves (except on

days like today when she is expecting someone).

When she was pregnant she was so full of desire that she was ready to explode, and lay in wait for Mr Rice everywhere. Now she leaves it to the tulips to impregnate her, now she rides the roses...

Mrs Rice
Nonsense, give me a man.

Narrator
One night she dreamt that she saw Hitler looking down at her from a poster on the wall, who in his odious voice shouted: 'You must not masturbate!' She hadn't planned on it either, she thought in the dream – she had grown tired of it.

Now the car rolls up the drive, now she pulls off the gardening gloves, now she adjusts her hair and pulls Ellen up from the grass, now the suburban housewife with the delightful child with dark curls welcomes the family's new nanny, and now we hope the suburban housewife does not have dirt on her lips after copulating with the flowerbed.

Viv
That's the lady who saw me collapse after receiving word of his death the last time we were together, now I'll have to show her my strong side.

Narrator
In order to avoid unnecessary confusion: the following events took place approximately one week earlier.

Viv
The phone rang. Mrs Rice answered and handed me the receiver. I had not heard Aunt Alma's voice for years. I stammered. I have never stammered before. I stammered the word 'father' so many times that she lost patience and shouted 'Yes, he's dead, and you might as well know straight away that *I* have removed both of you from my will.' Then my voice finally stopped skipping – it was the notion of money that settled it, that returned it to its senses, but only for a moment, before the stammering seized on 'how'. And while 'how-how-how-how' threw me out of joint I knew that I was stammering to postpone my understanding of the message I had received; that this skipping gave my mind, my soul, my consciousness, my old head time to prepare for the shock; I sensed the noise, the shock got closer, then it was on top of me and landed directly on my head and caused my knees to buckle. Mrs Rice, whom I barely knew, slid a chair beneath me.

I asked how it could have happened. It wasn't difficult, my aunt responded. The cold and the booze. His heart had stopped one night under a bridge. But I thought he was in Florida. No, he had travelled north.

That was not accurate, I later discovered. It was an out-and-out lie. He lived in Queens. He had been found dead in his apartment. His wife Berta had died a month earlier.

'Yes, you have lost a father,' Aunt Alma said, 'but I have lost my little brother.'

I don't know why she thought that was worse; she must have insight into a hierarchy that I'm not familiar with.

He is dead, not as a man of seventy-six but as an entire series of men, of all the ages and all the temperaments I have known: the friendly one, because he was sometimes friendly, and the disgusting one; the man who forced me down onto my brother's lap, and the man we waited for at the front door because we hoped his coat pockets were bulging with misshapen candy taken off the production line. And the drunken bawler who could sound as ugly as Hitler in the German I never learned. I learned Mother's language, not Father's. And he was also the man I was afraid of getting separated from in the throng of people when the police forced their way through the crowd with Langley Collyer's corpse. And the man Mother made me sing the Daddy song to in order to make him stay.

Father is marching towards me in all his forms.

Alma was not the only one who had removed us from their will – our old father had done the same thing. He left us nothing 'for the reason that I have not seen them in many years and that they have not been close to me'. Those words were written about Carl and me. He deserted me, he left me, I mourned for him back then. I am finished mourning. New chapter.

Aunt Alma

They had done him up nicely. Before we went in to see

him we were told that we must not touch him, or press against him – why on earth would we do that? – because then there was the risk of fluids running out, the nature of which I had no desire to imagine, though maybe it would just be pure alcohol, out of his mouth. 'Did you put make-up on him?' I asked. But what's-his-name hadn't, he had just washed him.

'It's your fault,' I said to Maria, 'you drove him from house and home. You didn't understand him, you French bastard.'

Vivian just stood looking stupid. She didn't even defend her mother. I couldn't understand why his face wasn't flushed and red-veined, that's why I asked if he was wearing make-up. He was pallid. I was nowhere near crying. I have to admit that I broke wind, silently, I could run the risk of doing it because they would all think the smell came from him. At this point we, the so-called immediate family, only get together at funerals – there are no weddings. Well, I suppose I was just rummaging through my purse, at any rate it escaped my notice that Vivian had pushed her way forward to the front rank and was now bent over him, as close to his face as she could possibly get, and started to photograph him.

'Vivian,' Maria shouted, 'you mustn't press against him.'

'Stop that at once, have you no respect for the dead?' I said. But she didn't hear a thing: she just continued, right up close. And that made him even more into an object, and I shouted that at her, 'He's not an object, he's still a human being,' but then I began to have doubts. Vivian had made him into an object. A moment ago, he had been a dead human being. Then she spoke to me: 'Grand-père offered Mother his name, but she didn't want it.'

'That's right, I didn't want it,' Maria said; 'I had at long last managed to shake off Maier,' – and she pointed – she actually pointed – at the bier – 'was I then supposed to hitch Baille to it?'

'We manage fine with the names we've got,' Vivian said.

'But he was always good for a laugh,' my husband said (we're not married; he doesn't want to, but nobody knows that). Imagine having been nothing more than good for a laugh.

There was a moment of tension: would the door suddenly fly open to reveal Carl standing there? But how would he have found out that the funeral was today, how would he even have found out that his father was dead? I saw Maria and Vivian steal a glance at the door more than once. And I wanted to shout at them, 'Do you two think he would even dream of coming? You managed to drive him out on the road, too, he's probably lying dead and bloated in a ditch somewhere...' I was on the verge of saying it, when I felt my husband's hand on my arm, because when it comes to me, he's a mind-reader. Joseph squeezed and whispered into my ear: 'On a day like this there has to be a limit to the malice.'

Then I remember that he is Russian, that he doesn't understand a thing.

All the same it surprises me that he wants to defend Vivian, I thought he still held a grudge against her after that telegram she sent to the Russian Embassy in '56.

But he has clearly forgotten that, so I nudge him and whisper 'Fifty-six'.

Narrator
'May you be haunted by the blood of Hungarians,' Viv wrote in French to be certain the Russians understood it. And it sounded splendid. So splendid that she quoted it several times. And then more fuel was added to the fire.

Aunt Alma
After the ceremony, we went into town together with the intention of going our separate ways, all suspicious of one another, I have to say, apart from my husband and I, obviously. The way Vivian stared at my fox fur. I remembered Maria's coat, she bought it in the forties when she and Charles entered the ring for another round even though he also had Berta, and he earned two thousand dollars a year, so she didn't need to work, but just went to the pictures, sometimes twice a day. He bought loads of hats for himself. And his shirts were sent out to be washed and ironed. Vivian is wearing the same style of clothing as twenty years ago, she never left the fifties. Her clothes look like they're from the Salvation Army, and they probably are, too. We part ways at a street corner; they know that I've written them out of the will, but I don't think we'll see each other again, and for a moment I am moved by this, which is why I bring it up again: 'And remember not to expect a penny from me, you have his death on your conscience, I don't know how you sleep at night'.

Vivian stood with that peculiar smile that I'm unable to decipher, and Maria had already turned on her heels. Then Vivian followed her, I took Joseph by the arm, and we stood watching them disappear, two women who looked like they were from another time, Joseph didn't think we would see them again either. I'll probably be the next to be shovelled six feet under. Then they had better keep away. Now I'm going to say what I once again thought when I stood looking at Charles. I thought: why all of this fuss? Why do generations have to pass and come and go? Why weren't there simply a finite number of people created from the beginning who were then immortal? Then you could avoid all of this bother with procreation (I've never taken the plunge) and death. I don't mention it to Joseph, because then I know I would be enlightened about his great borscht-eating Lord.

I resent there being someone who knows more about me than I do, here I am enjoying the springtime, thinking it's lovely, and that I'd like to be here next year too, and He's sitting up there with his abacus knowing that this will be my last year, or that I have exactly three springs remaining.

Maria
The sight of Charles at the end of the road made me think of the wooden signs in the French countryside where the roads divide: they stand in the landscape, pointing.

Narrator
So we're back where we left off.

Viv
There's Ellen, the slightly podgy child. It wouldn't be a stretch to say that she's sheathed in fat. It takes some effort to reach her. That's why I rap her lightly on her fat

cheek and say, 'Knock, knock.'

I'm just supposed to call them 'Sarah' and 'Peter'. They're liberal-minded. They can call me Viv. But Ellen has to say Miss Maier.

'We're probably about the same age,' Sarah said. I didn't respond to that.

'Thank you,' I said. 'I would like a large padlock, please. And nobody must ever come in here. That is my only condition. The room at the top of the stairs is mine.'

'No admittance,' I said to Ellen, and wagged my finger in the air.

The staircase is wide. It flows up. It flows down.

'And I would like to have the newspaper when you're finished with it, please. The newspapers, even – much better.'

Sarah is a journalist and subscribes to several papers.

Ellen shouldn't come running towards me from behind, she knows that now. I'm not Mary Poppins, like she thought. They had told her that now she was going to have her very own Mary Poppins. I have explained to her that this neighbourhood by the immensely beautiful (and today shimmering in the sun) Lake Michigan is different from the rest of the world, and every afternoon after school I want to show her all sorts of things that aren't found here. My day: 7 a.m. wake Ellen, make sure she eats her breakfast and gets on the school bus. Grocery shopping. A little cleaning but it just gets dirty again. At 1 p.m. pick Ellen up from the school bus, make sure she eats her lunch. Then look after Ellen, and that means: take Ellen out in the world. Make dinner to serve at 7 p.m., then bathe Ellen and put her to bed, unless Sarah feels like doing it. But I prefer to be told that first thing in the morning if that's the case. Off on Thursdays and Sundays. Sarah and Peter have separate bedrooms. They've got the child they wanted. Peter has made work his god, for Sarah it's work and the garden. They hope and believe I will make Ellen my god. I intend to make her into a person just like me – free and independent, the way I see myself on good days. I say things as they are to my children. The truth gives you a thick skin, and without a thick skin you won't have a chance in this great vessel we call Life, you'll be scrubbed to pieces.

Narrator
Hanging in the wardrobe was a fur collar with a fox head and dangling paws. Over the years Vivian took several pictures of women with fox-fur collars; in some photographs it appears as though there is a conversation taking place between the dead foxes on the women's shoulders, behind their backs.

The house consisted of twelve rooms and three bathrooms. Vivian used her bathroom for developing. When an object made it up to her room, it never came out again.

A very beautiful light came in through the large windows in the hall, whose walls were painted a quiet red. And in the afternoons. She stood. Sometimes. For a moment. Outside of her room at the top of the staircase, with her eyes shut, and felt the warmth.

Peter
Vivian arrived one Sunday and made us her first meal, a welcome meal, on the Monday night. We simply could not guess what it was that she had served us, becoming

increasingly mystified the more we chewed. And she looked jubilant when we couldn't guess what the meat that was unlike anything I had ever tasted was. We had to give up in the end.

'Tongue,' she said.

I could see Sarah was about to choke on her mouthful. Ellen was by then already in love with Viv and behaved like a model child.

'Salted ox tongue.'

Narrator
Many years later, after having been with Viv day-in, day-out, with her revealing next to nothing about herself, Peter Rice gave some thought to the symbolism of that first meal, the tongue salted and devoured.

Peter
And with the tongue she served a dark, full-bodied red wine, an Egri Bikavér intended for us alone, while she drank water. We knew that she came from France, you could also tell from her accent, and that she thought Americans smiled too much – and showed their teeth too much. She always smiled with her mouth closed. And then there's the fact that she was a non-practising Catholic. Neither then nor later did we discover anything else about her.

Ellen
I did *not* think she was Mary Poppins – she has no umbrella. She walks very fast and swings her arms. I have to be careful not to get an arm in the head.

Narrator
That's right, long strides and swinging arms, paddling across the troubled waters of the mind.

Viv
Today I photographed a pigeon resting on a cornice, blinking down at the streets. In my version it became heroic. Because it took in the streets with its small gaze. A little later, outside the station – someone must have dropped some food because a grey sea of pigeons surged upon the same spot; a fresh wave arrived and bored into the crowd, and here and there a wing flew up above the competing mass resembling a sail – feathers were flying. The nausea came at once, I had to go behind a shed and throw up. A little while later when I squeezed through the hectic crowd of people in the ticket hall and over to my platform (where all of us in our grey and dark coats were congregated, a few lit up by scarves with a little light and colour; if someone had thrown a diamond necklace into the air, and it had landed on the floor between us, we would have fought for it, with sleeves and collars waving about) the discomfort was over.

As a child it seemed incomprehensible to me that something could happen when I wasn't there to see it. That now serves as a kind of solace in relation to death; I mean that one day I'll no longer be able to see what's taking place, but all the same so much has taken place that I haven't seen that I'm used to it, so it's probably not that bad.

I thought about André Kertész's photographs of pigeons, in Paris and in New York – well it doesn't matter where because all pigeons look the same. It is difficult from his photographs to determine what are pigeons and what are their shadows, all just dark voraciousness. In one picture there is a man sitting on a bench with his back turned, and the pigeons (and their shadows) draw closer to him. I can't look at a bird without thinking that if I were dead it would hop on top of me and hack into me in that uncomfortably inattentive bird-like manner, every other moment looking up and glancing around, strips of flesh dangling from its beak, then another hack, look up, as though it didn't give a damn about the desecration of a body, as though it were just something it did *in the interim*, whilst vigilantly surveilling its surroundings. I do realize that it's keeping an eye out for enemies. But to simply be eaten in that absent-minded manner!

Sarah

Ellen and Viv were standing in the doorway about to go out when Ellen said to me: 'You don't like the Ellen who goes for walks with Miss Maier. When we get home, you'll be gone.'

'Why, that's not true, Ellen,' I said. 'I was the one who wanted Miss Maier to come live with us and take care of you.'

'Well, then I want to tie you up.'

'Balderdash,' Viv said and grabbed Ellen's hand.

'You're welcome to tie me up,' I said, and so she ran out to the garden and fetched her skipping rope and tied me to the chair where I sat with a frightful tangle of knots. Meanwhile, Viv stood in her coat shaking her head: 'Now I really have seen everything!' she said.

I wriggled free after they had left, but I was sure to be in position under my bonds when they came back. I wanted to be someone who could be counted on.

When they returned home and I was set free (officially), Viv said: 'I've spoken to Ellen. This won't happen again.'

The other day when I got home from The Paper, Viv had dragged Ellen's old stroller out of the garage and stood in the driveway wiping it down with a cloth. She says that Ellen walks so slowly that it would be easier to wheel her around.

'Viv,' I said, 'she's six years old! You'll just have to walk a little slower.'

She got so angry that her entire body was shaking. 'My name's Vivian,' she said, then grabbed the pushchair and gave it a proper shove, sending it careening into the middle of the road, but she certainly didn't care, she simply turned her back to me and stormed into the house. I fetched the pushchair myself and put it away. When we met in the kitchen later, her upper lip curled towards her nose in a kind of smile, and I said: 'That's quite a temper you have.' And she was clearly used to hearing that a lot. Maybe we should have cleared part of the basement for her instead of placing her at the top, I'm afraid that the elevated position has given her delusions of grandeur. She still hasn't put out any of the old newspapers by the garbage can, but I suppose she hardly gets a chance to read them. I don't know if I should feel guilty about her having such a long workday, but we're enjoying our nights out. At times I can almost see Peter as a stranger again, though I did have a funny dream: I became aware that I was having relations with the young apprentice, which came as a surprise to me. Well, one morning I stepped into the editorial office and saw that there were signs with our names by our seats just like there were on all the children's desks on Ellen's first day of school. I went over to my seat and turned my sign around: it read Ped-Ophelia. That was my name now. I turned around and found Peter standing behind me with what I can only characterize as a sardonic smile. 'You shouldered that well,' he said. And I replied: 'Well, I do come from the city of Big Shoulders':

> Hog Butcher for the World,
> Tool Maker, Stacker of Wheat,
> Player with Railroads and the Nation's Freight Handler;
> Stormy, husky, brawling,
> City of the Big Shoulders

Clearly, I didn't tell Viv about my dream otherwise she would have dropped dead by the stove – but I did teach her Carl Sandburg's poem, which was right up her alley. Later I discovered that she had taught it to Ellen, and that Peter, on hearing her recite it, had commented in a didactic tone: 'That was in 1914, that's no longer the case.'

Peter

Building worlds where life can take place, for however long it lasts – I'm speaking of decorating the home and landscaping the garden. For periods it has taken up so much time that I have thought that what should be the background (for our lives, for us) has become the foreground. I look at the new carpet and think: does it represent me? And the flowerpots on the patio: are they there in order to say something about me? I assume that we get rid of the ugly things so that they don't point back to us. Having bad taste, that's almost worse than being a stupid pig. Presumably I take it for granted that we decorate things for the sake of others, not for our own. Maybe because I trudge through my home with blinders on, and if I spot something I don't like, I just position myself so that it is out of my field of vision.

Viv
I'm off work. The world is open to me. Resting against my stomach is *the house* which is briefly inhabited by various people. They are mute. The only thing you know about them is what you can see. I'm in the silence business. I'm in that business because it is silent.

Narrator
She shoots from the stomach. Taken from below and pointing upwards. Endowing the people she captures with a certain magnitude. Making even the bums appear somewhat majestic, at least those that are still able to stand.

Viv
Some like having their picture taken, others don't. Many don't even realize it. But I take them whether they like it or not.

This is the only thing in the world that never makes me impatient. With this I can solve any problems that arise. There is nothing to despair over, because I know what I am going to do; I don't always know straight away, but it's just a matter of keeping at it for long enough. The vacuum cleaner, on the other hand, which is defective, can make me beside myself (I don't like asking Sarah why one minute it is sucking and the next spitting everything out), and I have to struggle with the filthy beast day-in and day-out. But there is *one* similarity: as a menial I ought to be invisible and go largely unnoticed in the streets so I can take my pictures in peace.

It's true that I quickly get very angry when people throw stones in my path, so that I can't move at the tempo that suits me – that's the only bad thing about children, that they walk so slowly. I feel sorry for dogs whose owners force them to walk glued to their leg so that they can't move at their natural tempo, which is generally at a gallop, just like me.

Narrator
What about the children and their natural tempo?

Viv
Ah-bah, I'm teaching the Snails to keep up. How grimy it is when you get outside of Wilmette! In this part of the city the streets are full of garbage and rats. Even that which once was alive is simply shoved down the gutter.

Narrator
One night in '66 you can see Martin Luther King on TV shovelling piles of garbage that have accumulated in one of the lanes in the city's South Side. The next day Mayor Daley sends the sanitation workers out to clear garbage *in that part of town*. By repeatedly responding promptly and tangibly to King's requests he avoids taking a stand

on what King's campaign in Chicago in '66 is all about: racial discrimination. Another example is the 'Hydrant Riots'. The summer of '66 was hot. In the summertime, the residents were in the habit of opening the fire hydrants and letting the children splash in the water. That summer, municipal workers enter several of the black neighbourhoods and turn off the hydrants, and fighting breaks out between workers and black residents. The police get involved, and the fighting intensifies. Daley asks King what he would advise him to do, and because he is worried about the immediate situation, he simply urges Daley to turn on the fire hydrants again and give African Americans safe access to swimming pools in white areas. And so Daley does. He has an entire lake at his disposal. He opened the hydrants and had sprinklers connected, and he had portable swimming pools driven into the black areas. The water gushed. 'They hope we grow gills and swim away,' one of the civil rights advocates said.

Viv

Here lies a cat, made flat by death, partially covered by a flyer and withered leaves. It gave me an idea. When I came home, I buttoned my blue velvet coat over a white blouse so that the very top could be seen, and spread the coat out on the patio with the arms out to the side and placed my red hat above the collar, so that empty, flat Viv lay there looking tired and dusty. I continued for some time using flatness. My shadow served well here. I felt my way along by placing leaves as the vital organs in the shadow's chest, heart and lungs. At times it just looked like extra seasoning.

I also allow my shadow to fall upon people and take

photographs with my shadow elbows jutting out. I become part of their world without them knowing it. I have lowered myself into their lives.

Narrator
Vivian did not begin in earnest (that is to say *incessantly* wherever she stood, taking along first her Brownie later her Rolleiflex in one edition and then another edition and soon several around the neck at one time and later still other types of cameras, I don't want to go into detail with the technical side, don't expect words like exposure time, darkroom and contact sheet from my mouth, at least not very often – all the same, it was fascinating to read Man Ray's description of his conduct in the darkroom, how he used materials whose expiry date had long since passed and broke all the rules of developing, and how from that came extraordinary results) to take photographs until the late forties, when she stopped seeing her father/when he stopped seeing his children/when father and children stopped contacting one another. Was that why? Father is gone, in future I (Viv that is) am going to preserve everything of significance that crosses my path. I *have* it in the can, my lifetime suitcase dangling down by my navel, my leather animal, my Rollei. It has been made into mine. It cannot disappear from me.

(It is my task to find plausible explanations, motives, reasons, it is my excuse to exist).

Viv
That was when the grandmothers died.

Ellen
When we are at the beach in Gillson Park that Miss Maier and I love so much that we're there almost every day, she keeps her clothes on, including the coat if it's windy, but she has her legs out (with hair she calls fur). Then she stands by the shore watching me and looking like a bird, taller than normal because I am floating on the lake looking up at the sky with her face on it.

'Why do you take photographs?'

'It clears my mind of everything else.'

'But so many?'

'It's better to look outwards than inwards.'

'What do you mean by that?'

'The world is more interesting than my brain.'

'You do it constantly.'

'I'm constantly spotting something.'

'Can I too?'

I can, and so can Joan, so we photographed Miss Maier and one another in that amusing world.

'Careful careful' she shouted every time we passed each other her Rollei.

When I get out of the water, and she towels me dry, we pretend I'm a meal she is cooking, and that she's mixing in all kinds of things. I'm also the pot, and every time she rubs me with the towel, we take turns shouting out the new ingredients she pours in: flour, salt, forcemeat, horse droppings, grass, tongues and pepper, and then she stirs my hair one last time. The meal is finished, I'm dry.

Narrator
I've never been to Chicago – I'm hindered by my

handicap which I am not going to bore anyone with – but I've bought a second-hand laminated copy of *Streetwise Chicago* on Amazon, which doesn't get crumpled or tatty, and it folds up, and I have found both Highland Park and Wilmette (and I also stumbled across the Obama's Home, but I can't find Gillson Park in Wilmette), and followed Vivian on the routes she took to take photographs when she left the suburbs: around The Loop, to Maxwell Street Market (on Sundays) and down wild, dangerous Madison Street.

It has never been easier to write about places you have never visited, one click and you soar above people's houses, though there are many pitfalls and you can really put your foot in it, place mountains where it's flat and things like that, which is why it's best to refrain from descriptions. And by and large I've done that, too. I say 'Chicago', and then it must be Chicago.

It's 1968, the Vietnam War is raging, there are violent race riots after the assassination of Martin Luther King, thousands of African Americans pour out onto the streets of Chicago's West and South Side looting shops and setting buildings on fire, nearly every building on a three-kilometre stretch of Madison Street is destroyed, the West Side looks like a war zone, eleven people are killed, hundreds lose their shops and over a thousand people are made homeless. Viv arrived a couple of days after the rioting and took photos of the devastated neighbourhoods and the national guard patrolling the streets.

Vivian is totally absorbed by Robert F. Kennedy's election campaign, and since she is thousands of kilometres from the Democratic primaries, she has to document them by photographing the front pages of newspapers that have to do with Kennedy's campaign – and in the end, front pages that have to do with his murder.

Viv
The elephant, the largest and noblest of all the stuffed animals, is RFK, and Ellen has placed it on a toy wagon that she slowly pulls down towards the play house that is St Patrick's Cathedral; Sarah and I form the procession, the slow tempo all the way through the garden makes me cry (I can't stand the tempo, and I can't bear that he is dead, either), which pleases Ellen to no end because she saw a lot of people crying on TV, even though she doesn't understand how you can cry over someone you don't know.

Narrator
The Democratic National Convention was held in Chicago from 26 to 29 August in 1968 with the purpose of nominating a presidential candidate, the party is divided as regards the Vietnam War, Vice President Hubert Humphrey is nominated (and later loses to Nixon). At the same time as the delegates arrive in the city, thousands of activists pour in, and again violent riots and clashes break out between anti-war protestors and the police. The press calls it the Battle of Chicago. Mayor Daley has armed the city to the teeth and ordered the police to shoot-to-kill arsonists and shoot-to-maim looters. There has not been such a heavy military presence in an American city since the Civil War. Miraculously nobody is killed, but the tear gas flows, and the fighting swells in the streets so that people are pushed through shop windows.

Vivian takes Ellen with her to Grant Park to photograph the protestors, but Ellen gets so scared of the police and the large crowds – 'Can you get shot buying ice cream?' – that they have to return home.

From that day:

> Officers lined up
>
> A small sharp-featured woman, elegant as a silhouette, teasing an officer with no appreciation for it
>
> Pigs kill (graffiti on a wall)
>
> Young protestors, they're lying on the grass in the park, they're sleeping, they're reading the paper

Sarah
I don't know why I didn't dismiss her, even though what she did was appalling, and according to Ellen she has done it before. When I asked why she did it, she replied that these interminable meals made her lose her patience, because she longs to set off, out in the world. By which she means the streets. And she cannot tolerate throwing away food. She thinks it is wrong when there are so many poor people. But Ellen is fat, I said, even though Ellen was sitting right there, and I regretted it afterwards – obviously I should have had that conversation when Ellen was not present, but I was honestly so shaken that I didn't think about it. She doesn't have to eat everything, that's how excess weight is established, you destroy her ability to notice when she is full, I said. She herself stood and was so long, lean and flat underneath

her loose clothing. It is coercion, I said, my child is not to be treated like that. Nobody should be treated like that. She nodded, and then she did what she often does when encountering opposition – she slipped away. That's how I would describe it: she retreats inside herself even though she is standing right next to me. She slipped away, and then marched out of the children's bedroom with her lengthy strides and swinging arms. There was tomato soup and dumplings everywhere. Ellen had stopped crying, she sat sucking on her hair, she always has to have something or other in her mouth. Something went very wrong in the oral phase – she never left it – maybe I should have nursed her a little longer. Viv gives her far too many candies. If she didn't get so many sweets over the course of the day, she would probably eat her meals quicker.

The door was open, and, when I walked past out in the hallway, I saw her standing bent over Ellen, and I didn't understand what was going on. She had practically forced Ellen's head into her armpit – I think I must have thought that Ellen had maybe got something in her eye and went in to see if I could help. They didn't hear me come in – not until I stepped into the room did I see that she held Ellen by the nose and was forcing a spoon into her mouth. Ellen's head rocked wildly, and she was kicking out with her feet. When Viv heard me, she let go, and Ellen opened her mouth and threw up and coughed and cried. Instead of going directly up to her room, Viv first availed herself of our bathroom, she let the water run for a long time, she probably gave her hands a proper going-over. In fact, I know she did, because the nail-brush was wet. I feel like a spy. I suppress my urge to open the door to her room with my spare key when she is not home. This curiosity regarding her life gives me a feeling of inferiority, and that was also why I didn't dismiss her; I feel in a way that she is above me. It's ridiculous – I'm her employer, and she is completely dependent on me and the envelope I give her at the end of the month. A little later I saw her walk past in the street, with the box on her stomach.

And we thought that we would finally have a little peace after the succession of nannies we have struggled with. The previous one had severe anaemia (it turned out) and was always so tired, every day after lunch she fell asleep with Ellen on her lap, and when I came home late in the afternoon, they were both sound asleep, but then obviously Ellen couldn't sleep at night; the one before that (and that was a pity) had hit her head falling from a tree and was not exactly age appropriate, it was like having a big kid in the house, she missed her mother and comfort ate and then just shoved the dirty dishes under the bed and left them there; and then there was Susan who rode strangers' horses in the paddock during the night, I caught her in the garden early one morning with spurs and a bridle in hand.

Later in the day they played out in the garden, Ellen was with the children from the road, and I received confirmation that I had been right to keep Viv. They were down in the wild part of the garden. She filmed them, but when I came out of the house, she started to film me. We never ever get to see any of the many films or photographs of us. When I ask, she always says that her things are in disarray and she can't find anything, or if I press her, she promises to look for them, but nothing ever comes of it. I'm not entirely sure if I like that. The children lay behind the shrubs pretending that the shrubs were houses, they held the large leaves up in front of their faces and knocked from inside – I think they were pretending to be apples. Finally, they tumbled out of the bushes, bursting with laughter, and Viv said: 'I think I'm going to make apple sauce out of all this nonsense.'

Viv

Let's bring it out in the light, so it doesn't remain secretive and grow dangerous in the shadows, in total obscurity: before I started to stuff food down her gob, I sensed the evil pass through me, it came alongside me and cut me off the road by turning in front of me. It added an extra profile, so I suddenly could be seen in three profiles; that is, with the evil as the third.

I would really rather not add more evil to the massive amount that already exists in and emanates from this country. But the evil entices and carries me off. I want to be rid of myself, I want to put myself down.

Narrator

At this point I happen to think of one of my first days on a drama course I took when I was young. The teacher had a couple of large suitcases with him, and when he turned them upside down (he was probably gentler than that), a colourful array of masks were revealed, and we (the students) were asked to each choose one and put it on. I chose a blue half-mask. Then he told us which masks we had chosen. Mine was a (blue) phantom spirit. He encouraged us to look in the mirror with the mask on, and the mask, which left the lower part of my face free, drew attention, as I saw it, primarily to the lower part of my face, which no longer looked like it was mine – I could see both my father and my grandmother in it, and rather than feeling possessed by something wild or unrestrained, I had become possessed by my family, by Jutlandic soil. Well, then we had to find the mask's sound. Mine didn't say very much. But you can bet that its counterpart did, a red phantom spirit that the oldest student in the class, a woman in her sixties, had put on. It practically screamed. Then the teacher said that now we had to see what the masks wanted from each other, and the red phantom spirit started sniffing at me more and more intensively until it suddenly knocked me, the blue spirit, onto the floor, because even at that time I was delicate, and launched itself on top of me and started to perform something that resembled mating. The teacher had to use force in order to manage to separate the red spirit from the blue one and to get me back on my feet.

Mrs Rice
You allowed yourself to be overpowered by a sixty-year-old woman? Was she a soldier? A police officer? Was she employed as a security guard?

Narrator
I think that's where the game ended, and it was clear how things could go when the masks took over. The elderly student's violent conduct was one thing, another thing was my brutally exposed lower face, the way I was tormented by my family for the rest of the day; I would say that is the closest I've come to a psychotic experience: that my relations had taken up residence within me and

were not easily expunged.

Sarah's psychologist
I've started to think of memories as Thought Phantoms.

Viv
Caroline from the camera shop asked if I wanted to come round to her place and see the moon lose its virginity, well actually she put it like this, 'see the moon get dragged out of its virginity', but I couldn't make it fit in with everything I had to get done that night, I didn't see the landing *live*. So for me the moon is still a virgin. Besides, I haven't visited anyone (other than Mother naturally), I mean *strangers*, since I visited Nicolas Baille, also called Grand-père, and I didn't really like the thought of stepping into a home without having to carry out a job there. It suits me far better to have a chat with her over the counter, at the shop.

Ellen
When we're in town, first we go into the long store and all the way to the back, to the candy, where there are free samples. Miss Maier has brought her purse with her. I keep watch and tell her when all the shop assistants have their backs turned at the same time. Then she dumps the whole tray in her purse. We get one piece from her purse every time she takes a photo. She takes a lot. The purse is usually empty when we get home. Her father once worked at a candy factory and brought candy home for her and her brother. He was the one who made sure that the machines worked so that the candy turned out

right. The candy that looked wrong, he was allowed to take home. But he didn't tamper with the machines so that they produced misshapen candy that he could take home, because then he would lose his job, and no one would get any candy. The misshapen candy didn't taste any different. It could have been a gummy bear without a head or sugar dusting, or a chocolate coin on which the year couldn't be made out.

Viv

My masterpieces from Champsaur have surfaced again. I can't think of anywhere I have *not* looked for them, but nobody's been in here, have they? And the moment I found them I sat down and wrote to the photography lab in Saint-Bonnet – so that I didn't have a chance for second thoughts. I told him that I have quite a lot of interesting things lying around, a huge number in fact, and things where I have tried a bit of everything. In short, I asked him whether he was interested in working together, whether he would make prints for me again. I remembered to write that he should use the same paper as he used for the postcards. It turned out so well that time. And he lives so far away. Things would not get confused. The person I am here and the person I was there. And in a way, neither would the photographs and myself. He would not see me when I had to deliver the films, he would just receive them in the mail. It will be terribly expensive. I am not in the least certain that it can be done.

Then there is the question of style and choice of subjects: do the pictures point back to a certain person, to me? I ponder that every time I have been to an exhibition.

How much of the person behind the camera can be seen in the works? Is one hidden behind them or on the contrary do they unveil you? I think they do. The narrator is the real main character.

Narrator
I can only agree with you.

Viv
My latest unforgettables:

> Burnt-out armchair on the street, cloud of smoke hanging above
>
> Woman in flowing white dress, around the neck a cape of silver fox, heading towards her flashy American car, night
>
> Audrey Hepburn
>
> Well-dressed plastered dwarf being led away by an officer and a man in evening wear, they have him by the arms, but have to walk bent over (dwarf's triumph)
>
> Two elderly people, are they siblings, are they a married couple, he is well-dressed, she is wearing an extremely crumpled nylon dress, he leads her off (could Carl and I have shared our life in a sisterly brotherly way – I was definitely the one given the task of carrying him away). I often see people being led away – on the way to a prison, on the way to an institution – and it fills me with dread.

Fat Polish woman talking threateningly to a police officer, she has thrust her face right up to his

While I wrote the letter, Saint-Julien became so vivid for me. When I inherited the farm from Aunt I did not for a moment doubt that I should sell it, I was not going to be part of this little gossipy community where everyone knew more about you than you yourself did.

Beauregard lay in a bend, with its back against a forest and its face overlooking the land. I sold it off, bit by bit. In the end only the farm remained, left to face all its losses.

Sarah

I've started to see the garden as a mind or a psyche or a character, maybe my own, with weak points and strong suits and cravings and aversions; that might be a bit on the extravagant side, but when I reflect on it, it's perfectly clear to me, in that case the weeds are an expression of... yes naturally: perseverance, not accepting a rebuff, immediately getting up when you've fallen, that sort of thing. Then there is the rose garden that nearly had Peter demanding a divorce because it demanded so much of us; the roses, my craving for the mysterious, all these perfect twists and turns which constitute the rose, the unicorn of my garden. There are several ways that I could describe the cherry tree to Peter so it would not disturb him. I could say: to me it seems to be somewhat Christ-like. Then he would ask: How? And I would be able to say a little about the exposure it exhibits, that it looks faltering and vulnerable. If I put it bluntly: 'It is a matter of time before the other trees set upon it, our Christ-tree which this year for the first time stands with its crown full of berries,' and he would fetch a blanket and shove me down on a chair and speak of too much reading and long days, the effect of poor sleep, and while he wrapped the blanket around my feet he would say that the only ones who are out to get something here are the birds swinging in the treetop to get the berries. But I wish I could tell him everything exactly as things are. I can, if it concerns the modestly simple and hardy hollyhocks (from the seeds Mom brought with her from Denmark some time ago) which sprout up all over the place between the flagstones on the lower patio, so we sit in a forest of tall swaying perfectly fresh newly arrived flower faces, namely: Peter, we must never rebuild the patio. There is no other patio in the country that looks like this. It is completely original. But that is not the way I feel like talking to him. And that is not the kind of thing he feels like hearing.

Soon I will have been a mother for a long time, I notice it most when I look at Ellen's things. The clothes change size, the bike gets swapped for a bigger bike. Then there is a new school year. Time goes by, but when does life begin? I rarely speak to Viv, she is usually too busy to sit down with me in the garden, and as soon as she gets a day off, she leaves the house. I don't like to ask where she goes. Usually it's just the garden and me. How do you build a relationship with a person who has no desire to talk about herself? I am accustomed to familiarity arising through the exchange of information about one's past with another person: a bit of a childhood and a flourish from a love affair, there you are, so what have you got for me that can shed some light on you? But I can't meet Viv that way. If I am lucky and catch her on the right foot, I can get an analysis of the latest movie she has seen, or we can talk about what we've read in today's paper, but that's how it is with me – I'm a hound for intimacy. When I most hate myself for that, I see myself as someone who basks in other people's confidences in order to bind them to me.

Viv

Everything blossoms lavishly, the bumblebees seem twice as big as they normally do, and there are wasps. Just now one of these oversized bumblebees landed in the grass next to my and Ellen's blanket; it is really two to three times the size of an ordinary bumblebee; the impossibility of it taking flight – I got it to crawl up on the newspaper and carried it over to a shrub and set it down high up (the leaves gave way dangerously under its weight) from where it then launched itself in death-defying manner, but it could not stay in the air and sunk into the garden. We tried several times, the bee and I, onto the paper over to the shrub, the leap into the air, the wings whirring, without being able to keep its body up, but at least they are able to act as parachutes and set the body down on the grass in a soft and secure landing. In the end I left it alone; a deliriously lurching machine between the blades of grass.

I am overcome with thoughts I haven't had since puberty. I am overwhelmed by wonder and strangeness, I don't understand what I am doing here, submerged in this enclosure of time that is my life, or what everybody else is doing here. And words like life and world mean nothing to me. It comes easier when I pretend it's not strange; then I can talk a little about the bumblebee. I take a deep breath and see whether it can't rectify my being out of step with the world.

Sarah
When I walked past the flowerbed with the metre-high foxglove (also from the seed Mom brought with her) one of them struck me on the shoulder like a penis, an accolade, like something from a forgotten world, a world where you can stay in bed with your loved one for an entire day and delve into each other; where you have been asked to dance so many times that you are weak with happiness and can no longer move. The window is open, and the forest or the lake outside has moved in and has settled over you – that's how heavily you've rested. Oh, such a long time ago.

> A Bee his burnished Carriage
> Drove boldly to a Rose –

Ellen
The little kids on the street call Miss Maier 'Army Boots', because she has such big feet and wears robust men's shoes. It's because men's footwear is practical, without heels, it's necessary because she walks so much.

Viv
And now look at what is taking place: A bumblebee has been feasting high up in the hollyhocks and has now landed on my thigh, its lower body is yellow with pollen – now it performs a kind of gymnastic exercise in order to shake off the pollen: it stands on its forelegs and shakes its hindlegs in the air. And afterwards it stands

on its hindlegs and fences with its forelegs... I'm starting to doubt whether it can even fly in its heavy pollen suit, so I blow on it, sending pollen flying into my face. It takes off and is gone! Maybe it's hiding in the pleat of my dress.

Last night I woke up to an incomprehensibly disgusting sound – at first it was incomprehensible, then it dawned on me that it was the large brown moth trapped in my room, now clattering around down by the skirting boards, seemingly weak, in the process of drying up. I encountered it for the first time when I switched on the light around 9 p.m., and it shot around bewildered and covetous. Over the course of the summer I have taught myself to free butterflies. When a butterfly hits the windowpane in an incessant belief that the windowpane is air, I capture it in a glass and slide a plate between the windowpane and the mouth of the glass so that the plate forms a lid – and then a rescue to the heavens.

Ellen

We're not allowed in the long store any more. Someone saw us taking all the candy, and we had to give it back. I think they just threw it out, because I didn't see anyone pour it back in the bowl. There was also lint from her purse on some of it. But then why couldn't we just have kept it? Miss Maier said it didn't matter, she had been thinking of buying me an ice cream anyway, because there was something we were going to celebrate. I couldn't eat dinner, but Miss Maier never gets cross at night, because then I just have to go to bed. Miss Maier said that we were celebrating the fact that she had been with us for exactly two years today. We all toasted to a long life for us all and with Miss Maier in the house always.

Viv

Hull House: the weather was truly awful, I was out there alone walking around like a phantom, taking my pictures and thinking about the other phantoms, the emigrants who had left their small dark rooms, if they had not been lodged here at Hull House, who had come for a bowl of soup and a glass of milk and a bath and English lessons and sophisticated lectures about various interesting subjects by professors who made themselves available free of charge on Sunday afternoons at Hull House, it could for example, as the case was in 1903, be a lecture about the Lake District in England or a recital of Euripides' tragedy, *Alcestis*. I took a picture of myself, so that I could see that I was not an old emigrant phantom fluttering through time, but stood there with my big feet.

Sarah

Now you might think that today you are going to hear about my round-cheeked companion, my chubby eight-year-old daughter Ellen who does not want to sleep and eats too much, I said mentally to my psychologist, sitting in his waiting room, considering what I was going to divert him with this time, but no, I said to him, still only in my thoughts, no you're not, you're going to hear about me again, about the time I myself was a round-cheeked companion, probably around ten years old, but I'll probably keep the best part to myself, which is that sharply drawn scene inside me of my grandfather, who, shortly before I went back home to Chicago after one of the numerous holidays I spent in the house with them in Denmark, pulled me aside and asked me to follow him into the bedroom. I knew perfectly well what was in store, because it happened each time I left: he found his brown leather wallet on one of the top shelves of the built-in wardrobe in the bedroom where (on the same shelf) the important documents also lay, among other things, the deed to their house their bankbooks their passports. I knew that from all the numerous times these important documents were taken down from the shelf during fierce thunderstorms and taken into the living room to join us as we awaited the outcome of the storm – on the sofa, above us, a painting of a mighty sailing ship sweeping off under a darkened sky – ready to hastily flee the house with the documents in hand if lightning struck the thatched roof, since the house, precisely because of the thatched roof and the old dry beams, not to mention the old crumbling walls, would quickly catch alight. This is connected in my mind to the fact that upon purchasing the house they had found large quantities of old clothes buried out back when they started to dig up the garden in order to landscape beds of flowers, but first and foremost vegetables, and especially potatoes – that goes without saying – their primary source of nourishment; and quite early on I had my own patch in their large garden where I cultivated the same things as them, just on a lesser scale, and so I also cultivated potatoes, primarily, but also leeks, onions, beets, peas, strawberries, and after every single meal we readily agreed that the crops from my patch of the garden, these vegetables I brought home, that is to say these vegetables which I drove along the flagstone path from the furthest reaches of the garden and into the kitchen on my yellow wagon, we agreed that they tasted best. And one time when I thought I had pulled up the long root of a carrot, it was the tail of a dead rat, not a carrot, that I pulled up. I just want to add that the greatest object of fascination in my childhood was a book cover that depicted a stylized landscape (stylized to the extent that, for example, the treetops were shaped like green balls), consisting of – besides these trees – a river, many different fields marked in different colours, and an oh-so-brown road meandering through the landscape which I could never tire of slowly running my finger along – I don't remember if there was a house at the end of the road – whilst enjoying the billowing cornfields, the meadows, and the river that flew past. To settle down and journey through a miniature world that matched the size of my finger, a world that consisted of blotches or areas of different colours, yes, that was a little like driving my yellow wagon down the flagstone path in my grandparents' garden.

Now I have to loop back to our present garden, my two thousand square metres of earth, where my round-cheeked companion last poked up her sad little head; I had rashly had an area of one hundred square metres cleared of bushes and scrubs in order to add this patch to the already large lawn, and I now pictured a row of brightly coloured shrubs forming a fence up to the neighbour's after all this boring brown shrubbery had been cleared away. I, or my occasionally numb soul, have developed an addiction to bright colours, and I am often on the verge of buying some completely meaningless object as long as it is red, yellow or orange; I saved a yellow snail from the road, the grey ones I left; and in a corner of our kitchen, out by the patio, I have hung up several colourful posters of tulips, roses and poppies respectively, so I can plant myself in that corner and take a heartening and bracing colour shower.

'Well, it isn't risky art,' Vivian said at the sight of the posters. 'No Vivian,' I said or should have said, because I said nothing, 'it's not art, they're flower posters.'

'What's that you've hung there?' Peter asked when he came home from work, and when I explained to him that it was meant as a provision to warm the soul, he said nothing; but I could tell that he thought these posters reflected bad taste. Let me also mention that I have placed scented soap bars among our clothes and bed linen, and though now there will be no more confessions it might be an opportunity to mention that to some extent I am afflicted by a need for openness, and that I have possibly inherited this openness from my mother, even though there were times I suffered when she opened up, whether to me or to a virtual stranger; I seem to be under the notion that I have a quasi-obligation to give a detailed account of perfectly private matters to complete strangers, that I have to make a report about what strictly speaking only concerns me. As though I owe them that, as though they expect it, even though in reality they would probably prefer to be spared. Living day-in and day-out with Vivian, who is quiet as a clam about everything concerning her life, has made me more attentive to that side of myself. I remember that my mother wondered about this need within herself which she was nevertheless incapable of combatting – she continued unabashed along the road of open speech, and the same goes for me, apparently. My mother was born in Denmark, less than one hundred kilometres from Germany. And instead of seeing her openness as a personal psychological phenomenon, it could be viewed as an ideal that came into being in the light of the uncanny silence that gripped Germany after the war. No, that's a bit far-fetched, to put it mildly. She would vehemently object to that theory. I don't know what I'm thinking. She was forty in '45 – did she suddenly develop her openness so relatively late in life? No, she was frank as far back as I can remember. Openness is quite simply a family weakness or eccentricity, at any rate a characteristic of the family. Sorry for persisting in embellishing this. My mom hates it, by the way, when I 'embellish'. There was however something she never or very rarely talked about. Which is what has led me to think about Germany. And, by the way, I am happy to admit that I have Germany on my mind – the other day I dreamed about Hitler again. She once said that it was – yes, what adjective did she use: maybe 'curious', to contemplate the notion that if her mother and her, both of whom have occasional psychotic episodes, had lived in Germany under Hitler, they would likely have been killed because they were mentally ill. I would like to make it clear that I am not attempting to connect myself to this gruesome episode from history in order to inflate my words with significance or give them greater weight, I said in my mind to my psychologist.

Well, the sight of this barren patch of earth billowing like a sea made my heart sink in my chest; two tonnes of roots had been removed, the gardener told me; now I had to rake and remove rocks, branches, more roots, dead leaves, before I could roll the patch of ground, rake it and plant some grass. I had decided. I'd do it myself. That was when my round-cheeked companion poked her sad little head up. I was overwhelmed by the task at hand. I felt completely alone and helpless as a child, standing before the wilderness. What I had initiated was senseless. Finally, I fetched a spade and a rake, hedge shears, a wheelbarrow and gardening gloves, got down on my knees and started to sift through this enormous amount of soil by hand, enormous viewed from a kneeling perspective. It took a week. All the while I thought of Jewel in *As I Lay Dying*, who singlehandedly clears forty hectares of land for the neighbour, during the night, by the light of a lantern, in order to be able to buy a horse which he then by turns strikes and whispers ingratiatingly to.

So there I lay rooting through my rich earth like a truffle pig, on my knees, shovelling dirt with my hands, the shovel long since abandoned as too coarse a tool, and, gradually, as the work progressed and I became completely enthralled with this ground-clearing work, it was as though I managed to force my round-cheeked companion back into the past, where she belonged.

And while we sat there on the sofa, my grandparents and I, I had all the time in the world, all the livelong night, because it was always the nightly thunderstorms that were the worst, the most ill-natured, those where it hailed so much that the windows were smashed in and the calves killed on the fields, to look at the documents and realize that apart from a couple of wallets, there was the deed to the house, their birth certificates, the marriage certificate, their passports and some foreign currency, in all probability lira, as they had once travelled to Capri. So I knew that brown wallet with spaces separating the notes, like walls between stalls which separate horses. These objects seemed to me to be a kind of essence of the two, my grandparents on the sofa next to me, and at the same time the chest in which the objects lay seemed to me to be the heart of the House which we had to save should the house burst into flames. There was also a smaller, well-worn, rather small purse with a clasp. It was a shade of black and looked like the one the milkman had hanging around the neck, and the ticket inspector on the coach had hanging down over the hip, but this was smaller, of a similar colour, and was used for coins. That wasn't the one he took down from the shelf. While my grandfather slipped his fingers inside to get a note, I adjusted my face to the right amount of enthusiasm and gratitude. 'Thank you,' I said, 'thank you so much, Grandfather.' 'Now show moderation,' he said, 'put them in your passbook, you have to learn to save, and don't tell Grandmother.' 'No,' I said enthusiastically, 'I'll be sure not to do that.' A moment before I had been through a similar scenario with my grandmother, in the living room, or out in the kitchen, where she had dug out a note from somewhere on her person (she was an outright monstrously physical person). When I was a child, she spat unhesitatingly on a handkerchief and with the help of saliva wiped chocolate and such-like off my face, so that I got the impression that despite our nice clothes we belonged to the animal kingdom. Now I can't quite believe that she pulled the note from her brassiere, as it was called back then, and I think she had probably taken it out of her apron pocket – even now so many years later I know her body by heart. It was milky-white – and very well-preserved, said my mom who washed her and dressed her for the funeral when she died, exactly what she was dressed in I don't know, but I know from my mom that, by washing her mother's body, she demanded almost more of herself than she could fulfil, to grapple with this body, white and soft because it had never seen the sun, the maternal body containing the now extinguished maternal mind, which she had fought so terribly with throughout her life.

'Don't tell Grandfather,' Grandmother said when she

handed me the note with a loving expression on her face.

(Just like the cloth bag with a nozzle at the end that my grandmother filled with whipped cream when she was going to make scalloped edges on the birthday cake and write congratulations on the cake; the emptier the bag got the further down towards the tapered opening her hands slid, until the last of the whipped cream was used and the bag hung empty and sticky over her arm – that was how I now wanted to squeeze out the last recollections of these people, until I have emptied my memories, if that can ever happen to me).

To this very day I've thought that she said 'Don't tell Grandfather', because he was so thrifty, and she didn't want him to resent me for the fact she had given me this note, the five-kroner-note (it was by the way also a five-kroner-note that he had given me). Only now, sitting in my psychologist's waiting room, do I realize that she knew his ritual with the wallet in the bedroom and did not want to deprive him of the joy of thinking that with this little ritual he had performed a unique act. The concealment of her gift to me was in fact out of goodness towards him, and not, as I had thought until this moment, a heeding of his thriftiness, so that he would not grumble about it, because for long spells they lived like cats and dogs, but only during the day. Every night they made peace, an agreement prevailed between the two to reconcile every night, that the sun must never set on an argument, here stretched or extended to the very pitch-black descent of night over the bed, where every night they then fell asleep, hand in hand. I know that because, until I was eight or nine, during the holidays I spent with them, I slept between them, and their interlaced fingers rested on me, or rather on my duvet.

If I am able to come to so many realizations in the anteroom, I thought, what insights await me then when I step inside – what should I call it? the consultation room? – with my psychologist. Or, as they say, the devil lies in the detail – maybe insight is found in the anteroom.

Narrator
We open our mouth and out comes... ourselves. I got an illustration of this, though that was probably not the point, when I saw the opening of Miley Cyrus' 2014 concert at Forum in Copenhagen, on YouTube, where first a massive three-dimensional face of Miley Cyrus appeared, then this giant Miley opened her mouth and a red chute was lowered out. Shortly after, the living Miley Cyrus appeared in the giant replica of her own mouth, slid down the chute, and landed energetically on the stage, born from herself, a virgin birth, by which the most over-sexed offspring imaginable had come into existence – no sooner was she was born than she showed every indication of a desire for reproducing herself anew. (Such an entrance demands an exit of a similar scale: hours later Miley Cyrus left the stage riding a red hot dog – this sounds like something out of Angela Carter's magic circus, or like Major Kong famously straddling the bomb). But that's beside the point. We open our mouth and out comes ourselves. That was what wore me out and for a time at least drove me into the arms of the silent photographs.

Ellen
I'm never going to have kids, it seems like they're only trouble. I have to go to New York City with Miss Maier,

she has to take care of something. Mom and Dad are away for seven days, they didn't want to take me with them. I saw them kissing in the garage, and they called the trip 'a romantic getaway', and each other 'lovebirds'. But first we have to pick some flowers. Miss Maier hides behind the cars in the driveways or out on the street, sometimes part of her is protruding, I can't have all these flowers in my hands and run back and forth and give them to her. In that garden I dropped an orange rose, but they don't have orange roses growing there, and soon someone will think: I wonder who has left an orange rose here, for me, right in the middle of the garden path, is it my lovebird? Now it is a large bouquet. Miss Maier has scissors with her and cuts the ends equally long, she does that while we walk. Afterwards she wraps a wet newspaper around them. I am allowed to rest my head on her shoulder on the train so I can sleep. She points at some men working on the tracks and remembers a poem which she thinks I should learn by heart. It's a train poem.

> THE DAGO shovelman sits by the railroad track
> Eating a noon meal of bread and bologna
> A train whirls by, and men and women at tables
> Alive with red roses and yellow jonquils,
> Eat steaks running with brown gravy,
> Strawberries and cream, eclaires and coffee.
> The dago shovelman finishes the dry bread and bologna.
> Washes it down with a dipper from the water-boy,
> And goes back to the second half of a ten-hour day's work
> Keeping the road-bed so the roses and jonquils
> Shake hardly at all in the cut glass vases
> Standing slender on the tables in the dining cars.

Our flowers are wrapped in wet newspaper, and we

eat fish in the dining car that has brown wood on the walls and oh-so-white tablecloths, and the waiters' black hands poke out of sleeves that are even whiter. Miss Maier is drinking ice coffee. She loves it. She gives me small mouthfuls from her teaspoon. She is mother number two. She describes to me a photograph she took last winter, when she saw three empty sunbeds on the beach; she went down to them and formed a snow figure in each one. Then she went up on the terrace she came from and photographed it. I had my sled with me. I arrange the napkins like the sunbeds, and my fingers walk around them, imitating Miss Maier's long legs.

We have taken several trains, and it is an entirely new day by the time we walk through St. Mary's Park. This is the park Miss Maier cut through when she was a child, when she and her mother visited her brother and father who lived on the other side of the park, the man and the boy both called Charles. They had split into two camps because the apartments were so small. Now we enter a staircase. It smells of sweet tinned goods, peas and pineapples. The door handle moves, and then bells on the other side of the door ring. There seem to be a lot of locks, and the bells ring and ring. The door opens. The lady takes the flowers, turns around and walks into the darkness. Maybe we're meant to leave now. We're not, we're meant to follow her, but first I touch the bells that are tied to a yellow string and hanging from the door handle. Miss Maier says that the bells are the lady's dogs – they bark if anyone tries to come in. The lady is French. She points to a stool on which I can sit down. She speaks my language to me and her language to Miss Maier. I can see her bones through the blue dress. I would like to go home now. Then I get some red powder in a cup, and Miss Maier pours water over it and gives me a spoon. It fizzes, it's raspberry. Miss Maier has to take care of something somewhere else in the apartment. I would prefer not to be alone with the lady. I have tried to keep myself from crying for a long time.

'When Vivian was little, there was no consoling her when she cried,' she says in my language. 'Is it the same with you?'

The tears fall on my knees because I have pulled them up to my chin.

'She made herself completely stiff,' she says. 'I would say to her: "I would like to help you." And how do you think she replied? She was four years old. She replied: "You can't." How do you think that makes a mother feel?'

Miss Maier returns, and I think she is telling the lady off because I'm crying. She hands me a handkerchief and says that it's perfectly clean. I don't think it is clean, but my throat and my head hurt from crying, and I want to stop. Miss Maier says to her in our language that now they are not to speak French any longer, because everything goes wrong in French; American is a calmer language. She says to me that we are going to spend the night there, and then the tears come flooding out again. Miss Maier points at the flowers on the table in a vase and says: 'Ellen picked them, they looked better yesterday.'

'They have been on a long journey,' the lady says. 'They're drooping a little, they are tired – perhaps they'll perk up overnight.'

But it must never become night.

We eat dinner in the kitchen, where instead of cupboard doors there are curtains, so that you can't see what is happening inside the cupboards, and which wrinkle up at the top. The paint on the pipes is flaking. There are ugly sounds coming from another apartment. We are completely quiet. Then Miss Maier points to the meat on my plate with her fork and says: 'I promise that soon I'm going to show you where what you're eating comes from.' Then the lady says to me: 'Vivian has never been able to get enough of reality.' I don't know how she knows all this about Miss Maier. I have to sleep on a yellow bed with black spots on it that they call an ottoman. I'm afraid to shut my eyes even though Miss Maier has left the door to the living room open a crack. I have to sleep in my underwear. When one of them speaks loudly, the other says shush. They are talking about Charles, who has taken the lady's name and is probably outside under open skies, maybe in Florida, because life is easier where it is hot. Miss Maier says that when it rained when he was a child, he was scared that the dead would fall down from heaven (did she really say that?), because he had seen how paste dissolves in water.

'Nonsense Carl, I said,' Miss Maier said. 'When we die, we disappear completely, how else would there be room for the next batch?' Now they both laugh.

'And the first time I put him in the zinc tub he screamed because he thought the water was black,' the French lady says.

She mimics him, 'I don't want to bathe in the black water I don't want to bathe in the black water,' and laughs unkindly.

I am eventually allowed to have the yellow string, the bells shout no no no when they are unwound from the door handle, the smallest in a thin little voice, the mother's sounds golden – her tongue slowly strikes the body. Now Miss Maier is talking about her masterpieces from

Champsaur which have been made into postcards, and the French lady says that she knows that she will never return there, and that it is a shame she left her Rollei there. But that on the other hand it doesn't matter, because everything has its time. Now the words on the other side of the door have started to become a piercing mishmash, I understand nothing, it's French, and I am scared that everything is going wrong, that we will never leave. Miss Maier keeps saying that I should look at the bells, and I do, but I don't like them any longer, they are cold stiff skirts where the real body inside is also the tongue. Now the French lady comes in carrying a candle, and if she is not allowed to console me, she'll get angry.

In the morning they tell me that I screamed, then fainted. But I don't care because now we're going home, and it was really stupid to have taken me along.

On the way home, on the train, Miss Maier says I will have to learn to like myself, because it's not certain that there will always be others who do. I don't believe that, but she nods and says yes. Then how do you do it? She says that everyone can find something or other inside themselves that they like. She says I have to close my eyes and find it. But I shouldn't tell her what it is. Have you found it? I have. (But there was a lot to choose from.) Then she says that I have to pretend that I am grabbing the end of something, and pull on it. The more I pull the more it unfolds, and finally it covers me entirely. That's what you do, she says, isn't that nice? Now the thing that you like fills everything. Yeah. Close your eyes and sit and enjoy it. I think it's so that she can photograph people on the train without me disturbing her.

Maria

When you get old, all you have is your steel helmet of grey hair, your age for a shield, and the bad conscience of others, the sense of guilt, to poke at. But Vivian is immune to that. Vivian is immune to most things.

I had a child who was completely different from me. She doesn't know what longing is. I think I can say for certain that when Vivian was young (no, she is no longer young), she never left a party and locked herself in a room and sat down on the floor with her hands on her temples, because she longed so wildly that she had to collect herself for a moment before she could again be with other people. She has never had any desire to have change and redemption come from someone else. And what is there to long for then, I mean really long for? And I don't mean longing for the workday to end, or longing to be back in Champsaur and the mountains, away from the sombre backdrop of skyscrapers that have never seemed real to me.

Nobody has touched me for years now, and in all likelihood nobody will ever touch me again. Not until my corpse is washed; I hope for gentle hands.

Sometimes I run my fingers over my throat and my cheeks in the most featherlike manner. And I have discovered that there are nerves in my eyelashes. I put black on them today and the mascara brush, yes, it tickled furthest in where the lashes meet the lid, I happened to think of Vivian who as a child asked if you could get cancer in your hair. No richness has replaced the richness there was (and is) in the past.

Viv

They hold hands, they fall asleep on the train and find rest on one another's shoulders, or they have their nodding heads support one another, the married couples, all the married couples, when they surrender to sleep together. I don't understand why anyone would expose themselves to falling asleep on the train. It happened to me only once, and I woke with drool running down my chin. I was always a bag of bones and nobody thought of calling me princess, nor could I ever have thought of calling Ellen or any of my other children that. Nobody is going to come and put the brakes on me, nobody is going to steal my life, even though I wonder what it will be like not to have anyone to lean against when I grow old, but there are after all no guarantees. Just make sure that you don't take a tumble from the big wheel of life – there is nothing more to do. I have never in my life seen a hand I would like to have close to me.

The high school boys buy sandwiches during lunch break and are already eating them on the way out of the shop. When I caught them on camera yesterday, it occurred to me that, even when I was a girl, I never wondered whether somewhere or other out there was the one for me. I don't think Carl ever had a girl, but he certainly could have had one without me knowing, because he would never have taken her home with him and subjected her to Mother or Father. I don't think so though: first he had the boys and the tricks, the cheque frauds, the reformatory, the prison, then came the drugs, six different types, then came the mental hospital, and then he was gone.

Sarah

'Sarah, Sarah!' she started to shout, from out in the garden, and I thought something had happened to Ellen and raced outside to the garden, but thank God nothing had happened. Viv was just enormously agitated about an experience they had just had on the train, where they had driven past some apartment blocks where the washing was hung to dry on lines stretching between the windows, and then Ellen had said: 'Look, Miss Maier, they have outdoor wardrobes,' because she had never before seen washing hung out to dry, but then Miss Maier also said: 'Ellen! Not all people have washing machines and driers like your mother. Some people wash their clothes in a tub and hang them out to dry on a line.'

And when she came home: 'Sarah, Sarah, it's scandalous that she doesn't know how the majority of people live.'

And she simply could not stop: 'It's a scandal, it's a scandal!' She kept saying it while she stood picking blackcurrants, she was so indignant that she was ripping and tearing at the poor bush, and I got scared that she was going to pull it up by the root. When she used the term 'rich ghetto' I went and put my hand on her shoulder and told her that was enough, that it was nonsense, and could she please stop crushing the berries.

Ellen

I have hundreds of glass animal figurines that I have bought in that little shop with all the clutter. Miss Maier also buys things there. She likes little things, just like me. When she has to leave a name so that they can phone her and tell her that the items she has ordered have arrived, she says that she doesn't have a telephone. She is allowed to use ours. But she has to give her name so they can write a name in the notes. 'Then write V. Smith,' she said. When we got outside, she said, 'You shouldn't tell everyone you meet who you are – remember that.'

Narrator

Vivian only calls herself V. Smith when she really needs some peace.

In documents they (authorities of every kind) have always got her name down the wrong way and spelled it differently: Von Meier, Maier, V. Meier, Meyer. So when you hear that Vivian sometimes spelled her name one way, sometimes another way, I would just interject that it was the authorities who started it, that they were the ones who inspired that practice.

Just once, upon her departure from France, Vivian became Vivienne and other times Viven.

Ellen

She has told me twice that she thinks the glass figurines are unhygienic and have to be washed. They are standing on my windowsill, the unicorn is the leader. The bear is the only one who can make him laugh and change his mind. The deer just do what they are told. In the afternoon she came in carrying a tub of water and a bottle. What is it? It's ammonia water. She pulled the stopper out of the bottle and poured it in to the tub. Then she held the tub up to the windowsill and swept my glass figurines into it. She was wearing rubber gloves, and she stirred them round and round. The animals thrashed about down there, clattering together. I know they can't stand touching one another. When I take them to school with me, I roll them up in cotton wool and place them inside a chocolate box, each with their own space, just like in a stable. Afterwards I didn't know whose legs belonged to whom. Miss Maier said I could pretend that they were ill and that's why they were lying down. I piled the legs together and pushed them into the corner. Miss Maier sat down on my bed and said she wanted to read something to me about how unhygienic it once was at the stockyards here in the city:

'It seemed that they [the meatpacking companies] must have agencies all over the country, to hunt out old and crippled and diseased cattle to be canned. There were cattle which had been fed on "whiskey-malt", the refuse of the breweries, and had become what the men called "steerly" – which means covered with boils. It was a nasty job killing these, for when you plunged your knife into them, they would burst and splash foul-smelling stuff in your face; and when a man's sleeves were smeared with blood, and his hands steeped in it, how was he ever to wipe his face, or to clear his eyes so that he could see? They [the plant owners] welcomed tuberculosis in the cattle they were feeding, because it would fatten them more quickly... They [the butchers inside the stockyards] would have no nails – they had worn them off pulling hides; their knuckles were swollen so that their fingers spread out like a fan. There were men who worked in the cooking rooms, in the midst of steam and sickening odours, by artificial light; in these rooms the germs of tuberculosis might live for two years, but the supply was renewed every hour. Worst of all, however, were the fertilizer men, and those who served in the cooking rooms. These people could not be shown to the visitor – for the odour of a fertilizer man would scare off any ordinary visitor within a hundred yards, and as for the other men, who worked in tank rooms full of steam, and in some of which there were open vats near the level of the floor, their peculiar trouble was that they fell into the vats, and when they were fished out, there was never enough of them left to be worth exhibiting – sometimes they would be overlooked for days, till all but the bones of them had gone out to the world as Durham's Pure Leaf Lard!'

When she was finished reading, she said: 'They certainly could have used some ammonia water, couldn't they?', and then she grabbed her Rollei and took a photo of the rubber gloves on the windowsill, where they lay looking like a pair of evil hands (Miss Maier said they looked helpless), and added that now we were going to go and see the slaughterhouses, as they were going to shut soon, and I had to have a chance see them before. But first she showed me an aerial photograph, so I could see what an enormous area the slaughterhouses cover. She calls it the animals' concentration camp, but says that it is nevertheless worse for those who work there. I walked as slowly as I could to the bus, because I hoped she would say that I was probably too tired, and that we had better wait until another day.

We're not going inside. It's not allowed. I didn't know that. But I'm happy about it. We stand looking at the pens with the fatstock: they are large and there are a lot of them, and there are a lot of animals in each one. So many pigs are butchered there that the city was once called Porkopolis instead of Chicago. And many cows were slaughtered, a whole lot of chickens, and some horses. In a short time, the sheep standing there will no longer be able to stand on their feet, but will have to lie down. Their bodies will be chopped into pieces, and the various body parts will be sorted and placed in piles. You can't eat most of their legs, only their thighs.

A sheep is already lying down, and the other sheep trample on it. I look at the sheep, and Miss Maier films it.

Now it's all over, and it wasn't as bad as I thought. It's dead. It died while I watched. And I stood here on the other side of the bars.

When we have to go home, Miss Maier says that she wants to take the opportunity to teach me to hitchhike. It's useful. I would rather take the bus. But no. So we stand by the side of the road and wag our thumbs, it's the same movement you use to jig cod, but sideways rather than up and down. We didn't have luck on our side, so we end up taking the bus anyway, but we will try again another day.

Ellen

I'm ashamed. I'm so ashamed that I stop being afraid of Miss Maier and grab her by the sleeve and say: 'No, you can't. Stop it, Miss Maier.'

She has positioned herself half a yard from a poor crazy man, taking a photo of him right up in his face without asking for permission, because she never asks for permission. She muscles in on other people with her vile Rollei, and when they get cross, she just laughs or shrugs and walks away or takes another photo. Why does she want to show someone that he is crazy? Why does she want to exhibit his poverty when she is always on the side of the poor? Why can't he be allowed to sit and be ashamed of being crazy and poor in peace?

Viv

Sometimes after we have eaten and I have done the washing up, and Sarah might have done the drying, they ask if I want to have a drink with them out on the patio. I don't drink. But I spend time with them. They might hold hands. They are liberal-minded, so they hold hands even when I am there. I see it as an opportunity to learn something. 'Now are you sure you don't want a glass?', Peter asks again, holding out the bottle for me. I couldn't be more sure: 1. I know how men get on a Saturday afternoon when they get paid. 2. I will not lose control and be different than I am.

We talk a little about the various neighbourhoods, how the occupants have changed over time, how people move on to something better when they can afford to, and how those who are worse off take over their homes until they themselves might rise up a little and move on. How the houses are emptied and then filled. Today I took Ellen to Cicero with me to show her and see for myself a place where, in '51, a black family moved into an all-white apartment building, which led to a mob of angry white people rioting. The mob was only quelled when the national guard was called in. It was in the papers and on TV around the world. Here in the city the racial struggle is fought over the housing stock. I stood thinking about how scared the family must have been, and how different they must have felt, such courage such perseverance such defiance. Their apartment building was set on fire and rocks were thrown at their windows. And the white fire department refused to direct their water hoses at the white culprits, which they were later fined for. I also showed Robert Taylor Homes to Ellen.

Narrator

The largest social housing estate in the world, four miles south of The Loop, consisting of twenty-eight identical sixteen-storey buildings, built in the early sixties, which housed up to 27,000 black Chicago citizens. Clean to start with, and attractive, the estate eventually became a so-called vertical slum. And in the end, it was in such a wretched state that it was torn down. In 1999, a study was conducted at Robert Taylor Homes regarding the significance grass and in particular trees have on people's well-being and behaviour – it is an obvious place to conduct the survey since there is a view of greenery from some of the apartment blocks and not from others. Out of 150 respondents, three per cent of those with a view of trees and fourteen per cent of those who look out on a lunar landscape of asphalt and concrete had threatened their children with knives or firearms.

Viv

'This area experienced a great influx of people after the great fire of 1871,' Sarah says, 'when one Mrs O'Leary's cow apparently knocked over a lantern that set a stable on fire, they say, and caused a large part of the city to go up in flames. It was an unusually dry summer and an unusually dry autumn in 1871.'

'You speak like a book,' Ellen says.

'Well, then you're also going to hear a small poem,' Sarah says, 'about the night of the fire.'

> Men said at vespers: 'All is well!'
> In one wild night the city fell;
> Fell shrines of prayer and marts of gain
> Before the fiery hurricane.

On threescore spires had sunset shone,
Where ghastly sunrise looked on none.
Men clasped each other's hands, and said:
'The City of the West is dead!'

'The things you know,' Peter says, 'and after the crash of '29 all the white people who are able to, flee from the city and settle in the suburbs.'

'I got it from my mother who got it from her father, they filled their conversations with rhyme, they walked around with a great reservoir of poems they had memorized about this-and-that subject,' Sarah says to me.

'In a way it brings conversation to a standstill,' Peter says, 'because when the rhyme has sounded, when the verse has spoken, there is nothing more to say about the matter.'

'Let's defy the power of verse and continue talking about the fire.'

Then, for some reason or other, they looked at each other in a sultry manner, so I got up and told Ellen that I was going to put her to bed. I didn't tell them that I knew quite a few verses by heart myself, as well as entire stories by O. Henry, which Emilie read out loud to me in the months when I was her little child.

Today I saw something I believe Edward Hopper would also have seen – the façade of a Chop Suey restaurant, darkened by a century of soot. I stood on a walkway, relatively high up. The restaurant was divided into small rooms. Some people were sitting in one of them. The others were empty. Two men. One eating, the other leaning towards him. What kind of meeting was taking place? There was both a sense of a neglected existence and a sense of fatefulness to it. Maybe that fatefulness *is* a neglect of existence, a neglect that is nobody's fault. It's just too late to change. Much like the houses, the way they are filled and then emptied, for a period of time containing one life, and then another. It ended up being a dark picture taken from rather far away, and it struck me how many close-ups I take; I have to work more with distance. Distance opposes individuality, and I don't think that I am particularly interested in the individual. But V. Smith, surely you would not go so far as to say that you only see the people on the street as representatives of social classes, would you? No, despite everything I don't believe that. Excellent, V. Smith, then let's leave it at that for now. Yes, because I don't know. Yes, Time. They represent Time.

Later today I pass a construction worker standing with his big mud-smeared bottom poking right up in the air, I took the photo from so close that it takes a second to figure out what it is you are seeing.

They have Ellen in common, but I don't know how much they think about it. There was a garden with an empty swing, and so there had to be a child, too. She was conceived for the swing. I haven't been keen on dogs since I was a child. But I think that I live on the edge of their fire in the same way: just like a dog, I don't always understand their signals, or what they mean by what they say. When I have to sleep everything appears in squares, framed, and I get no peace from the pictures I have taken. The people return. I don't know if I'm searching for certain subjects, and whether as a result others might escape my attention. I would hate for that to be the case. The axis that the world rotates on: to have or not to have. Where does the money come from? Some people have sacrificed themselves so that others become wealthy, and I cannot stop noticing the result of that sacrifice – flour and leather: the mealy faces of those working indoors (I myself could have had such a face) and the leathery hands and faces of those who have spent their entire lives outdoors. In Florida I once saw a man who hid his face in his hands in exhaustion or shame – first I thought it was my father, then I thought it was my brother – I think my brother is still vagabonding and living on the streets and has become a man with bare feet in down-at-heel shoes.

Narrator
Her brother Carl rode off a long time ago on a foreign name, the name William Jesard, though it's not that foreign – he already had the name William from Grandfather Wilhelm. So really he just poked his American middle finger into his mother's maiden name Jaussaud and rummaged and pushed until it became Jesard. He might have already changed horses again, and then they'll never find him. They're not looking for him either.

'You don't look for someone who doesn't want to be found,' Maria said.

'Then we're rid of him,' said Charles Senior, who in Austria was called Karl and in America Charles, yes Karl-Charles.

Viv
I rushed off as soon as I had taken the photo. And when I had gone to bed and was half asleep that night, I had a curious experience: there were two vibrating or whirring bodies secured to my body, one down by the feet and one

around the forest feast region. It was not connected with the tingling I get down there when I have seen particular things at the cinema, more like something eerie, and so I tore myself free of sleep, but as soon as I was about to fall sleep again the same thing happened – two creatures were attached to my body. When I managed to wake up fully, I got up and switched on the light and kept myself awake for a while, so that I didn't immediately slip into this sensation of being part of a double or triple exposure again. I know that it was them, my brother and my father, who latched on to me. Where meat comes from, some have sacrificed themselves – Ellen knows that now.

Narrator
What if you had just looked at Duane Michals' double exposures for too long before you went to bed?

You are really very agitated. Maybe you should try to calm down by tidying up a little.

Viv
Yes, it's getting crowded up here in my room, but I can't just tidy up *a little* in one drawer, then I would have to tidy all of them, vacuum and scrub the floorboards, wash the curtains and all the clothes in the wardrobe. And I don't have time for that. As for the newspapers, I have no idea where to start and where to finish, it was my intention to create an archive of:

1. murder, rape, kidnapping, arson, assault
2. political events

but I haven't had time to clip what I wanted to. Once in a while, I photograph a few of the important newspaper pages so I don't lose them. But the negatives are also in disarray. I no longer know what is on which sheet, and there must be close to 5,000 rolls of film now, and they take up room too. But the papers are the biggest problem.

Over here, the insane people Hitler wanted caught up in his net and burned run around in the streets until the police catch them and lock them up. I've noticed that their hair is always dishevelled. Twice in my life Carl has called me Sis. Today I took a photo of a short officer with a tall madman under his arm. The lunatic had rolled his trousers all the way up to his thighs, but then it was a hot day. And sure enough, his hair was dishevelled. Had I not photographed him his misery would have crushed me.

Sarah's psychologist
I like the idea (mine) that memories are phantoms of the mind, a faint reflection of a past event that appears in you.

Peter
When Vivian talks about the bad situation of others, victims of homelessness and poverty, her voice goes dark and reproachful. It ends up sounding like she is accusing those of us who she is speaking to. She makes it sound like it is our fault. And that merely by mentioning it she is personally placing herself on the side of those less fortunate. She makes us into adversaries, even though in the strictest sense we are often in agreement.

Only I think that maybe the expression 'the prisoners of starvation' is a little wide of the mark. Sarah says that Vivian would prefer not to go to the doctor because there are so many who cannot afford to. She calls America the grave of the Occident, we talk about the genocide of Native Americans, about slavery, about Hiroshima and Nagasaki, about Korea, and most of all about Vietnam, until I take Sarah, who has collapsed under the weight of the miseries, by the hand and together we escape into the garden.

Sarah

Vivian does not speak very nicely to taxi drivers. She doesn't have a driving license, and so we let her take a taxi when she has to do the grocery shopping. 'What's the idea?' I hear her say. 'Do you not have a watch or do you just not know how to tell the time, you should have been here half an hour ago,' and then she crawls into the back seat and slams the door behind her. She buys on the cheap or is simply given bruised fruit and tired vegetables which would have been thrown out otherwise. Naturally they're for her, not for us. She has a shelf in the fridge. When we have meat for dinner, she eats the fatty bits that the rest of us cut off because they're not healthy. 'You have to have something to burn off during hard times,' she says licking her greasy fingers, and I have to admit my stomach turns. She licks the wooden spoons clean before washing them – and yes, she also licks the pots.

It makes me recall my grandfather's as well as my father's thrift, how we measured the water in cups before we boiled water for coffee, so that energy would not be wasted on heating a drop more than necessary, how we saved on lighting, how all the packaging was washed and saved to be used later for another purpose.

Narrator

Some time ago, when I read an article about the Uruguayan president, José Mujica, the president of frugality, who raged against overconsumption, and is now retired, I thought about your father, Sarah, because the two of them remind me of each other – it could easily be your father photographed with an old thermos outside the modest house instead of José Mujica, who donated the majority of his salary to social projects and had the presidential palace put to use for the homeless, standing in a shabby fleece jacket. (Viv would have liked him, but she died the year before he became president).

Ellen

This Sunday Miss Maier forgot to lock the door to her room when she left. She keeps the key to the padlock on a string around her neck, hidden underneath her clothes – the string is so long she can feel the key by her belly button. She keeps the string that long so that she doesn't have to remove it from her neck when she unlocks the door. But she takes it off when she has a bath. The door was ajar. I saw it from the hall below. I went up the stairs. When I stood in front of the door, I nudged it slightly with my foot. I could see that there were a lot of newspapers inside. I nudged it a little more, even though I was really scared, and constantly listening for the sound of her moped. You couldn't see the furniture at all. I was last in the room before she moved in, quite some time ago now. We had left a bunch of flowers on the bedside table to welcome her. There was a bed, a wardrobe and a bedside table, and now you can't see any of them, not from out here where I'm standing. But I can see something resembling paths between the stacks of newspapers. It reminds me of a cemetery, the paths between the graves. Then I did something I shouldn't have done. I fetched Mom. And she fetched Dad.

Sarah
Strangely enough the first thing that occurred to me at the sight of all the newspapers was the start of Rimbaud's poem 'L'Éternité': 'Elle est retrouvée. Quoi? L'Éternité...'

Because here it was, and stacked formidably high, eternity; every single day (I assume) of the last I don't know how many years bundled up, time as something you can touch, and my hands went black from the printing ink; the eternity of days, the past, the lost time, the amount of life that has passed (under my nose, I'm tempted to say). Eternity. As the heathen that I am, I can only perceive eternity as the time *that has been*. It was frightening and pathetic. And horrifying. And in a way reassuring because time passes so quickly – I often get the sense that time is skidding away from me (I look up, and the leaves on the trees are already yellow), that I find myself in a landslide of time. It had come to a standstill.

As Peter says, it was dangerous. We have literally been living under a huge fire hazard. 'So this is where they went, all the newspapers,' he said afterwards, slowly. Yes, we've found them again! Then we heard the moped, she was on her way. Ellen got scared, she grabbed both of us and wanted to drag us away, she is big and strong, and we had to struggle a little to shake her off. For a moment, as she tugged at both of us and we fought back and collided, the three of us, we belonged together, we weren't saying anything, it was solemn and chaotic – remember this took place on the landing outside Viv's room, and we had to make sure none of us fell down the stairs – no, it turned into a completely mad circle dance. Suddenly I noticed that Ellen's body was now that of a grown-up, and the words flew out of me: 'Well, you are far too old to have a nanny.' 'No, Mom,' she said, 'no, don't do it.'

Then Viv was in front of us.

So we let go of one another. Peter's tie had ended up twisted around his back. It felt like she was our schoolmistress and we had done something wrong. When I bent over and forced my heel back into my shoe, it was only to postpone the torrent of abuse that had to come. But no. Viv stood there for a moment, then walked past us without a word and shut the door behind her. We went back downstairs. I felt elated and put my arm around the two of them, because together we had become real.

V Smith

I am hanging by a thread. The nest defiled by their gazes, my systems disturbed. It no longer matters about my room, now I can invite them up with their boots on so they can stomp on everything and destroy it all and spit and lie in my bed. Now I go down and say: You broke the rule. It was my sole condition. Now I have to tidy everything and start over. Now I have to take my good things and leave. Now they don't want me any longer. Now I pretend nothing happened, and it is going to continue as before. But I don't know if they crossed the threshold and wandered down my goat paths through the room and contaminated the cleanliness with their touch, or whether they remained standing on their side of the threshold and only let their eyes wander in.

Peter

Yes, imagine, it was as though we were paralyzed after discovering that we live in a house with a hoarder of such proportions. Suddenly she seemed very foreign and peculiar to us. It was Viv who took the initiative. She came downstairs and told us she would get rid of all the papers in one go. She would drag them down and out onto the driveway immediately and make sure they were collected and driven away as soon as possible. She also said, and she sounded completely despondent: 'There are so many things I haven't managed to clip out,' and I could see Sarah softening, like she was about to tell Viv that she could delay their disposal a little, but to be perfectly frank, no. I reminded them of the Collyer brothers, who had been crushed to death under the huge piles of papers they had amassed in their home. And Vivian said: 'Only one of them was crushed. The other one sat in his chair and had died from malnutrition by the time the police arrived. But I don't collect newspapers in the same way as them – I do it because there's just so much I would like to clip out and keep. I can't remember everything, nobody can remember everything they read.' (Here her voice went up and cracked). 'I leave what I need to remember on top of the piles so as not to forget it. But not everything can be on top.'

We offered to lend her a hand but she refused. Over the ensuing hours she ran up and down the stairs. It was quite the sight when she was finished – the piles in front of the house. Then you could see how much you had read. I have always read every paper from cover to cover, every day, all year round. I have kept myself orientated. I have tried to understand my time, from one day to the next. I have formed my opinions of it.

Vivian

Nobody is going to come here and tell me about Homer and Langley Collyer, I stood with Father that day in '47 when the police forced their way into their Fifth Avenue home through a second-storey window because all the doors were completely blocked. We had walked down from 64th Street where I lived, right up to the corner of 128th Street where they lived; we had stood in front of the house many times before, because Father was somewhat obsessed with them on account of all the stories circulating about them, and all the guesswork, more or less informed, about the treasures hidden in their barricaded house. Many hours went by from the time the police crawled in through the window to the moment they turned up again with Homer's body. We stood watching to see how they managed to manoeuvre Homer out through the second-storey window, and then carry him down the fire escape. He lay on a stretcher and was covered by a blanket, people were reluctant to move; I could see how little space he took up under the blanket. Later I read that he had only been dead for ten hours. He had died from malnutrition because Langley, in order to cure his eye disease, had placed him on a diet consisting of one hundred oranges a week. It had been many years since anyone had seen Homer outside, but Langley took good care of him, played Chopin for him, though I don't know which of the fourteen pianos he used – one of them had been given to the family at one time by Queen

Victoria – and he read out loud to him, and went out to do the shopping, and collected usable things, during the night, mostly, in the end, wearing a suit that was held together by means of safety pins. Father saw him one night! Homer lived in a small clearing between the piles of stuff. But they could not find Langley. In the days that followed, the floodgates of their palace opened, out flowed a rusted bicycle, a sawhorse, the hood of a horse-drawn carriage, a kerosene stove, a Model T Ford, all the pianos and all sorts of other musical instruments, his doctor father's collection of medical books and jars containing foetuses and instruments, he was something so odious as a gynaecologist, and his wife in fact left him, and all the tin cans, the rubble, the pieces of wood, the magazines, the newspapers, live cats – 140 tonnes of belongings in all. After three weeks' of clearing out, the workers stumbled upon Langley, who had fallen victim to one of his own traps which had been meant to safeguard them from burglars and authorities of all kinds. He was crushed to death by falling newspapers, and he had died only ten metres from Homer's little nest, his body in a horrible state, hollowed out by rats. (I picture the body like the house, with paths going through it).

They had an entire house with three storeys, a basement and attic that they filled to bursting point. I have only one room. And no inherited items.

Narrator
The things she hoards are connected; one thing leads to another, like thoughts, that's why she can't discard this or that object. Because then the chain breaks.

Ellen
Miss Maier has now cautioned me several times against men. She says: 'They put you on their lap, and then you feel something throbbing. Men are only out to hurt you.' Then I reply something along the lines of: 'Don't worry. When I grow up, I am going to live way out in the country and keep sheep and be as fat as I want, without anyone nagging me.'

But when she regards men in that way, I can see why she reacted the way she did on Sunday. We were down by the lake, and she had positioned herself on a toppled tree trunk in order to better capture her subject. It had been raining and the tree trunk was slippery, and suddenly she lost her balance. An older man who came walking along the path right behind her jumped over to support her. It was perfectly clear what he wanted to do, I stood watching it. She screamed so loud that it echoed, and jumped down from the tree trunk and hit him on the head with clenched fists. Somehow or other he must also have been struck by the camera, it must have swung into his temple, because he was bleeding. He said some horribly ugly things to her, but I don't know if she even grasped them, because she couldn't calm down at all. She was no longer hitting him, and wasn't crying, but she uttered a long shrill tone that just went on and on and rose and fell. 'Miss Maier,' I said, and put my hand on her shoulder, but that didn't help – she just kept uttering that sound while she shook her head from side to side. The man said he was going to sue her for assault. 'What is your name? You have to tell me your name,' he kept saying to Vivian.

'Then *you* have to tell me her name,' he said to me.

'I'll only tell you my name,' I said, 'my name is Ellen

Rice, she's my nanny (I didn't like saying nanny because I'm so old), we live right up there.'

Finally he left, and Miss Maier let me take her by the hand and lead her home. By the time we reached the house, she had fallen silent.

Sarah

Morning, on the sidewalk, in the slipstream of masculine fragrances – it makes me euphoric. But then I experienced something that nevertheless (at first) was a notch too far. I sat waiting for my psychologist in his consulting room and looked at the postcard of Freud's examination couch, which was hanging on his noticeboard; it looks straight out of an oriental dream, covered with an authentic rug and soft velvet cushions, a couple of velvet or velour blankets are slung over it, lying on that one would sink straight to the bottom (of one's self), my psychologist's leather sofa was a dismal failure compared to that specimen of furniture. I had plenty of time to breathe in the smell of the room. And it smelled, I would almost say stank, as though someone had been kissing in there for hours – it had the sweet smell of saliva, and skin that had been rubbing against skin for a prolonged period. The leather sofa. That must be where it happened. But this is a place for all of us wounded souls to speak: he should not use his consulting room for sex. I sent him a severe look when he came back, freshened the air around me by waving my handkerchief.

The next minute I thought: if he can kiss someone else here, then he can kiss me too. Now I was no longer a wounded soul but a smouldering volcano.

'Well,' he said, and sat down, 'now let's see if we can

get a little closer to who the person you designated as "my round-cheeked companion" actually is.'

But I did not reply. I let my lips hang invitingly, knowingly, wordlessly in mid-air. He took the bait. I stood up and measured him up by placing my hands flat against him everywhere, then I pushed him down on the sofa, and mouth to mouth we journeyed into the other one, the soft, the gaudy, the wild furniture. 'It's just me as a child,' I replied much later, when, completely dissolved and with skin stuck to the leather furniture, we untangled ourselves from one another.

'I see, well then we have located him,' he said.

'Yes, but it's a she,' I said, 'and I would like to be rid of her.'

'It is of no use pushing her away. Just let her come,' he said.

'She does,' I said.

'What's going on inside you now right now?'

'I am attempting to suppress a strong urge to throw myself on the floor and scream "No." I can't stand it.'

'Can you offer some examples of when the round-cheeked companion appears?'

'At the thought of or the sight of suffering I can do nothing about, wars, famines, epidemics, massacres, animal cruelty, schoolyards, and most recently she poked her head up from a big patch of earth I was going to clear.'

Then the psychologist talked about the necessity of finding a point of anchor, something to cling to, something that offered a foothold. It was a bad metaphoric soup, but rising out of this soup was my mother's infinitely dear face, and in future I would pound that into the head of my round-cheeked companion, almost like when you pound a tent peg into the ground.

Viv
Wouldn't it almost be strange if someone wasn't secretly photographing me? The man in the house across the road maybe? On good days I think he resembles Eisenhower, whom I had a certain confidence in and could never get myself to call Ike, as people were in the habit of doing. I thought it seemed clingy, wanting to be familiar with the president, or like he was a silly little dog.

What has always been difficult is more difficult now, like a kind of rheumatism of the mind, and I am afraid to think about how it will develop when I get old. I know I ought to visit Mother. I've started to keep the curtains drawn, so that the man across the road can't see my stacks, and I get changed in the bathroom. I have never seen anyone take a picture of me unless I've personally asked them to, yes, when I was a child and Mother did and Jeanne too. When I have asked someone to photograph me, for example Caroline, that day on the beach – then it's because I want to see how others see me. I have the beach picture on display at the moment, and there is something strangely vulgar to my face, like I've tempted somebody else out into the depths on purpose. But Caroline is the closest I've got to having a friend, and I almost exclusively buy film from her shop now. She is the only one who understands when I say that this community is an artificial world, a pinprick of grace and dignity. But I can breathe easier in the resentment and the filth that this pin is affixed to.

Ellen
Dad has taken care of it. She won't be sued for assault, even though the man got a concussion. Dad met with him, and I think he also wrote a cheque. For pain and

suffering. The day after the 'assault' Miss Maier told me that what I could learn from this was that I should not put up with anything, that attack is the best form of defence. I felt like reminding her of the time she held me by the nose and stuffed food in me like I was a French goose.

Viv

Are bulldogs in fashion? Are bulldogs the only breed a man can be seen with this year? It seems like I see men with bulldogs everywhere at the moment. I suppose by now you can call me a specialist in reflections – today I took an unbelievable picture of a black man with a white bulldog. He stood with his back against a windowpane at the station begging with a paper cup in his hand, and his masculine four-legged follower also sat with its back to the glass. Francis Bacon would have been delighted at the reflection: inside the glass the dog was completely warped, in fact in outright disintegration, and looked like a piece of falling paper. It was understood that the mirror is another world that does what suits it with us, drowns us and shakes us. That's also why I often make use of reflections in my self-portraits. I am fond of creating rows of reflections so the subject sinks into one world after the other.

The self-portraits are also a way of keeping a bit of an eye on myself, now that there is no one else to do it; well Vivian Dorothea, you have slept poorly again last night, the bags under your eyes speak their unmistakable languages. Isn't that coat getting too shabby, you'll have to see if you can afford another second-hand one.

And there I stand in miniature, far up in the surveillance mirror at the supermarket, tempted by all the products, the devil whispering in my ear: Cast thyself down and it will all be yours.

Narrator
You are not well versed in the Scriptures, Vivian. The second temptation of Christ is not about material gain, but about not smashing into the ground. The Devil has led Jesus up to the pinnacle of the Temple and says: 'If you are the Son of God, throw yourself down from here. Then your father will command his angels to come and lift you up in their hands.'

Viv
Rarely do I manage to capture myself smiling, but today I managed it: A man came walking along with a plate of glass, and I photographed him from behind so that I was reflected in the plate, and it looked as though he was carrying me.

Now I happen to recall the ice crystals on the church windows in Saint-Bonnet in February 1950, when I was waiting for the coming of spring, which meant soft earth, so that Aunt Maria Florentine's earthly remains could be moved. The others tugged at me because mass was about to start, but I couldn't tear myself away. I took as many as ten pictures, it was the shapes the ice made that admittedly unsurprisingly meant that from then on, my gaze was directed at buildings – yes, structures as such.

Sarah
Today Viv came by and showed me a photograph of Ellen from three or four years ago – I thought she wanted to give it to me, and I managed to say thanks *before* I realized that she wanted to sell it to me. By letting me pay for it she would ensure that I valued it.

'You decide how much you want to give. But you have to pay for it.'

As she said that, she held on to one corner, as though I might be tempted to run off with it.

'It's an intense picture, Viv,' I said, and it was. Ellen was on her way up a tall practically vertical staircase that led to a slide that was as winding as a serpent. She looked so very little by herself on the stairs, clinging to the railing. There were other parents there with their children, either on the way up the stairs with them or ready to catch them at the foot of the slide. But Ellen was alone on the precarious stairs. And why? Because Vivian Maier was busy photographing the scene. I had entrusted her with Ellen. And why wasn't I there like the other parents? There were fathers in the picture, it must have been a Sunday.

'You can tell how steep it is, can't you,' she said enthusiastically, 'how high it is!'

I dug into my purse for some money, and when I looked at the picture again, it seemed even worse to me. I looked at Viv.

'Art is not somewhere you feel comfortable,' she said.

I no longer thought of how I had left Ellen in the lurch on the crude metal staircase, which in my mind had become a picture of her entire childhood that I had voluntarily left in the hands of someone else; instead, I thought again of the passage of time and I was overcome by melancholy at the sight of the small figures climbing up, only to swoosh back down straight away.

Ellen

Joseph is so popular that he hadn't noticed me before the rehearsals for the nativity play started, even though our classrooms have been next door to one another these past four years. The lead parts had been given to those with really dark hair in order to make it authentic (even though you wouldn't think it was important when the donkey was replaced by a straw Yule goat), at long last I was advantaged by my hair colour, because I was to be Mary. The choir of angels were fair-haired – who knows what all those blondes were doing in the Middle East around year 0? I had two entrances and one line; the purple scarf that was held in place with hairpins kept coming loose. The pews were packed, Miss Maier was there somewhere, her soul's telegraph tapping pride and anticipation on her face. She doesn't say it, but I know she loves me. It seems like Joseph and the Wise Men got drunk during my first entrance where the angel told of the coming pregnancy and I did as I was supposed to: looked around in wonder and said, 'But no man has known me.' Because when I came back after the annunciation, Joseph lay on the floor with communion wafers over his eyes and an open mouth which the Wise Men also tried to hit with wafers. 'Hal-le-luja' one of them said to me. In a flash I understood the following: life is funny. But I could not dwell on it, because the matches were not there.

'I can't find the matches,' I repeated louder and louder, and at long last Joseph swept the wafers off his eyes and picked himself up and took the last swig of the

Communion wine. I stood with the candle waiting for it to be lit, which was supposed to symbolize the birth of Jesus. Every one of them was looking. 'Then we'll just have to enter with it unlit,' Joseph said. He took me by the arm, grabbed one of the shepherd's staffs, 'but then Jesus hasn't been born,' I whispered, because now we stepped inside the church, 'I'll think of something,' he whispered, looking into my eyes – it was strange to have his marvellous face so close to my own. He thumped the staff on the stone floor and invented an intense gait as we moved up the aisle and I carried the candle forward with both hands.

Narrator

When a baby arrives in a novel it usually has the air of being posted; it's delivered; one of the elder characters goes and picks it up and shows it to the reader, after which it is usually laid in cold storage until it can talk or otherwise assist in the action. Jesus isn't encountered again until he is around twelve years old, teaching the scribes in the temple in Jerusalem.

Viv

The man at the photographic lab in Champsaur never replied to my letter, maybe it never arrived, maybe he put it aside to reply, but forgot it or just never got it done, maybe he's dead. Maybe it's best like that.

I don't think Susan Sontag (who I wish I could get a glimpse of one day) is on the right track when she writes in *On Photography*, which I got hold of second-hand, that it's only with the work of photographers like Todd

Walker and Duane Michals that you can tell for certain they took the picture, because to a degree they specialized, the former with his solarized photos and the latter with his narrative photo series (I love the one of the child being abducted by a coat).

Caroline keeps pushing to see some of my work, it's possible that at some point in the future I will start buying film in other places, perhaps from now on a new place every time, or almost every time. What I produce is so good that if I start showing it to professionals, I'll never get any peace again. No one is going to see my room. No one is going to see my body. No one is going to see my family. No one knows where my brother is, twice he called me 'Sis'. I am going to keep walking and looking and walking and looking. I hope my heart stops one day while I'm walking, but that I fall in such a way that my coat or dress – depending on the time of year – covers my forest feast region. It's about time that foolish expression disappears.

Narrator
Dig your way through the tragedy and out the other side.

Viv
They had been drinking and grabbed me by the cheeks, which were chubby back then, and lifted me so that I hovered a few centimetres above the floor, and called me a white mouse and a young Mrs, but I was a Miss for always, because when they put me down on my brother's lap, I thrust my elbows into his chest.

'Such lovely trousers, Vivian.'

'They're forest feast trousers,' I said.

'But why are they called forest feast trousers?' Carl asked.

'I don't know,' I said.

'It's because they have wide legs without elastic,' Father answered.

'But why are they like that?' asked Julius Hauser, who was also there that day.

'Then you don't need to take them off when you're rolling around out in the woods,' Father replied.

I bit Father's hand, so they called me reptile, and I crawled through the corridor and into the kitchen with Mother, but she didn't pick me up from the floor, or else she would have picked up her own tragedy.

When I lay on the kitchen floor looking up at the cupboards that had no doors, but fabric gathered on cords, I noticed that the forest feast region, from the navel to the middle of the thighs, was also a cupboard. They had tried to open it to take something out, and now I lay here where nobody liked me because they hadn't been able to get it open.

If I were my brother, I would have changed my name too; he was forced to be a swine by the fatherstone (the stoneswine also known as the deceased), and he has bolted from the pigsty. New chapter: William Jesard, man with swine-free conduct.

But what should I call it then?

Narrator
The groin, pure and simple.

Viv
If people used all the time they spend thinking about sex thinking about justice, the world would look very different – stay a virgin throughout the sexual revolution, then things would get done. Simply run a comb through the hair and then off you go. Or a hat, then you save on shampoo.

Today I took a picture of a strip bar, standing outside were some people who could have been circus folk, but they were in fact some kind of sexcrobats, one was doing a handstand, and her dress had slipped down to the waist so her trousers could be seen; the other one, who was missing a shoe, was wearing a brocade dress and over that a man's shirt of the kind I like to wear; they stood under the sign that flashed its promise of a striporama into the afternoon, looking simultaneously cheerful and miserable. Only people as grubby as them would feel like touching their grubby faces and hands and breathing the grubby air that surrounded them.

Narrator
Maybe you should just dig into the memory of the Daddy song, then we'll be done with the incestuous or semi-incestuous all at once... What do you say...? Then it's over and done with, and together we can travel down less beaten paths. You might just happen to take an interest in the opposite sex, or what do I know, the same one. By the way, wasn't there a tall Indian in a supermarket in Las Vegas that you – with resentment – saw walk towards the exit and drive out of your life in a dusty pick-up? Dig deeper. I continue to find it a little bit odd that you love romances but shrink back from so much

as squeezing someone's hand; oh your still chaste lips, horizontal and vertical alike, because isn't it beautiful in French (which you mastered so quickly, but which always clung to your American, and vice versa: French coated with a thin film of American), *le sourire vertical*. Or, in order to contribute a little something myself: the lower smile. Upon what basis are you able to understand all these films that you see on your days off, Thursdays and Sundays, about magnetic fateful attraction between people (you who only invite people inside your box for the sixtieth of a second it takes your camera to take a picture)?

How can you free yourself from your parents if another loved one isn't deployed in their place? If you don't plunge into physical love, in which your entire existence is summed up, where you are hitched together, isolated, hitched together, isolated? Yes, I'm just asking. Well. Maybe it just calls for an extra-hard kick out of the nest.

Viv
Let me invite you inside a Man Ray photo from 1932. Unfortunately it's untitled, but I call it 'The Distorted Wheelhouse'. Very briefly: In a room with no straight lines... as seen through glasses with the entirely incorrect strength... the doors swell, the windows swell... a dark man with distorted features standing, turning a steering wheel... he turns a woman's face in a circle around himself. Maybe the whole wretched business or the *disruption* – the lack of straight lines – is because the cabin is full of water.

That's how it was when the Daddy song – 'My Heart

Belongs to Daddy' – came on the radio on the kitchen counter, in the old edition from '38, sung by Mary Martin. We're now in the post-war years, Mother and Father make another go of it, but it does not go well. Father has just left and slammed the door behind him, we hear him stomp down the stairs out in the stairwell, then we see him (from the kitchen window, Mother and I, at this point my brother has ridden off) appear downstairs on the sidewalk. Mother grabs my upper arm firmly, 'Try running after him. Sing the Daddy song.' Or maybe she says: 'If nothing else: then sing the Daddy song. Get him to come back with you at any price, daughter.' Or she says, casually, as though it is entirely irrelevant, because at that exact moment it comes on the radio for the umpteenth time: 'Go and sing it to Father.'

I don't understand why she wants him now when she was so happy to escape him in '29. But there is after all a world war between then and now – you look at yourself in the mirror in a different way. At least until it has again become a habit that you're alive.

Oh no – it must have been before the war.

Anyway, off I went – whenever it was. Down the stairs. Out on the sidewalk. Looked up at Mother, in the window. Across the street. Our house is situated on a bend. There's something special about them, houses situated on a bend. I mean on a corner. There he is. I grab his coattails, he turns around and wants to brush me off, but then I open my mouth and break out in song. I don't have a fur coat I can take off, a Siberian train station does not appear like in the musical, and the boys asking for more aren't there either, but I stand up and weave around him, it's Mother who is turning the steering wheel, I'm taller than Father, little Father, that won't do, so I have to go down on my square knees, so it's from down there that my heart belongs to him, Mother turns and turns, and I spin around Father dizzily until he says: 'Stop that,' but at that point I've got him turned (my storm my great Belgian horse my ship), and we return to the demented wheelhouse with Mother inside.

But the next time I didn't get him to come back with me – then it was definitive. A departure for always. It was planned; a bluish-grey suitcase swinging in his hand.

I never saw him feel pain. (The glossy drunkenness I don't accept.) I would have liked to see what that was like, just a glimpse of it. He was let off too lightly.

Ellen

Today something happened on the street, right outside our house. I was standing with Mom and Miss Maier in the garden watching. Joan's brother came cycling along, and a car drove towards him, then Joan shouted at him from their yard, and he turned his head and answered her, and because he turned his head, he accidentally wobbled and ended up in the middle of the road. The car hit him, and he flew over the hood and over the roof and did a forward roll and (at first) landed on both feet on the road (it was the craziest stunt), but then he fell and hurt himself. The bicycle was completely crumpled. We all ran out to him, his and Joan's mom also came racing over, and she shouted: 'God, I thought it was the dog that had been hit.'

It was nothing serious, he could talk, nevertheless, they called an ambulance. He was wrapped up in a blanket and had to lie completely still, and now the dog had also arrived – his mom hugged it, and you can see that in the photo Miss Maier took, and which she gave to me as a gift.

Sarah

Today Viv came and wanted to sell me another picture. Funds must be running dry. It's of me, from several years ago, where I stand in the schoolyard by a juice stand, and Ellen is sitting under the table. The party is over (whatever it was for, I can't remember). The schoolyard is empty and abandoned. I look tired and irritable but slim, and where are all the children, have they run away from Ellen, since she has ended up alone, curled up under the table? Apparently I was not worried about it, that is clear to see.

I shook my head, because I didn't want it. She didn't understand. Maybe she thought that here I could see that I had also taken part in everyday life in the torrent of memorable, or not in the least memorable, events such as a juice stand, that I had not just worked my life away or stood on my head in the rose bed.

Peter

Something really ugly has happened, not close to us, but in the vicinity: a babysitter and her own little baby have been murdered in an odious manner. Viv is preoccupied by it, and it's no wonder since it's someone like her it happened to. She came storming in (as though her life was in danger and she sought my protection) with the newspaper and put it down in front of me and smoothed it out, on the workbench, where I was making a shelf for Ellen.

Chicago Tribune

12 September 1972

MOTHER, BABY FOUND SLAIN

The beaten and naked bodies of a 27-year-old woman and her 18-month-old daughter were found yesterday morning in a church parking lot in Mount Prospect.

The woman, Mrs Barbara Flanagan of 5744 N. Meade Av. died from a sharp blow to the head or strangling, a coroner's autopsy disclosed. The daughter, Renee, died of suffocation caused by vomiting after she had been sexually molested. The autopsy failed to disclose whether Mrs Flanagan had also been assaulted.

'This is obviously the work of a deranged mind,' said Mount Prospect Police Chief Bert Giddens.

A six-man team of Mount Prospect police canvassed the neighbourhood around the Community Presbyterian church at 407 N. Main St. Both bodies were found face up in the church's parking lot. A gray blanket partially covered the woman.

A piece of electrical cord 2 feet long was found in the blanket. The cord could have come from the attacker's car but apparently was not a murder weapon because the bodies did not bear marks that would come from a cord, the police said.

Police were combing a forest preserve district near Milwaukee Avenue and Imlay Street where Mrs Flanagan and her daughter were last seen at 3 p.m. Saturday when they left a Milwaukee Avenue bus there.

Mrs Flanagan's husband Dennis, 30, said she was to meet a man who she said arranged earlier in the day for her to care for his invalid mother and two small children.

He said that his wife had posted a card on a bulletin board in a supermarket at 5700 N. Milwaukee Avenue stating she was seeking work as a babysitter. The man who called and asked her to care for his mother and children told her to come to an address that police later found was non-existent.

Mrs Flanagan told the man she had to take a bus to get to the address and the man told her he would meet her at the bus stop, her husband said. Before leaving she left her older daughter Laura, 7, with her father-in-law, Otis, who lives upstairs.

The bus driver told police that the woman and the child were approached by a man of about 30 years old at the bus stop and she and the child walked away with him.

The bus driver identified a police photograph of a known sex offender as the man he saw meet the woman. Police said he failed to identify the man at a showup, and he was released.

The bodies were discovered at about 7:20 a.m. in the lot by Donald Dittmann, 47, a sales representative who lives at 408 N. Main St, across from the church. The two bodies lay in front of the left front wheel of his car which he had parked in the parking lot.

Minutes before Dittmann found the bodies and called police, an anonymous woman caller told the Mount Prospect police that a mother and her daughter could be found in the lot.

A motorist who drove by an hour before the discovery, Kenneth L. Kranz of 413 N. Main St., later told police that he had seen another car in the lot.

Dennis Flanagan, husband of the slain woman, buries his face in his handkerchief as he is escorted away from the county morgue by his father, Otis Flanagan.

Viv

I'll start at the beginning: the bulletin board. Here, the commonplace prevails: someone wants to sell their bicycle, another offers to mow lawns (the murderer likely took Mrs Flanagan's note with him). The murderer stood here and caught the scent here, he smelled blood here and the plan formed in his head once he had done the shopping and paid and stood holding his stained net bags. Then I go to the church and walk around the parking lot – I have never been to a crime scene before, and I had expected a police cordon where the bodies had been discovered and maybe the police and curious onlookers snooping around, but there's nothing. All the same, my heart is racing. He dumped the bodies here, but where did the assault take place? I have my tape recorder in my purse, but there is nobody I can question. Why did he discard the bodies in front of a church, isn't that even more perverted? Some men have a thing for nurses and nannies, but why the baby too? Whenever there are really young children crawling around on the floor, I get scared of accidentally kicking them, so as a precaution I sit down on the floor and tuck my feet underneath me until that fear passes. Neither Donald Dittmann nor Kenneth Kranz were home, at any rate nobody opened the door even though in the end I got so impatient that I held the bell down, it was at Dittmann's that my ability to wait expired.

Now I'm standing in front of the house of sorrow. The curtains are drawn on both floors. Otis Flanagan lives on the top floor. Maybe he's in the right frame of mind to be able to answer a couple of questions. I think the curtain moves and I raise my hand with the bouquet. You have to remember that there is also a seven-year-old child – the father has something to keep living for.

Now the three of them form a small circle, father and grandfather will have to spend their lives filling in for the mother, maybe they'll need a nanny, but it's a modest neighbourhood, homes with no personnel. No one comes out of the house. I end up just laying the bouquet on the stairs.

I can hardly imagine something worse than being in the papers.

Ellen

The homeless call Miss Maier 'Kiki' (she told them that was her name) when we stop so that she can give them some good advice. She loves giving good advice, for example, 'I just saw an old mattress that was left out as garbage,' she says, 'if I were you, I would hurry over before someone else snaps it up. It's far better than your cardboard.'

Sarah

'Viv, I don't think this is working.'

'You don't think so?'

'No, I think you'll have to find another job.'

'You think so?'

'Yes, and look how big Ellen has gotten. We don't really need you any longer.'

'I seem to remember the other day you talked about how now that Ellen has gotten so big, you were thinking of getting a foster child. Couldn't you just take me instead?'

'That's not exactly what we had in mind.'

'I suppose not.'

Peter
My Lord I don't know how she has amassed so much stuff or what any of it is. It looked like there was a flea market in the driveway. Some of her possessions were in cardboard boxes, other things in handbags and plastic bags and plastic containers and even tubs. I was afraid that her new employer, Mr Marsh, who kindly offered to pick her up, was going to drive off in quite the hurry at the sight of it all. He came (sensibly) in a Land Rover, and together we managed to stow it all on the bed of the vehicle and lash it down.

Narrator
One of Vivian's photographs comes to mind. It shows a small family that has just got off the train and is standing next to all their stuff. The mother is holding a baby in one arm, two small children are standing next to her and the father, and they are surrounded by suitcases and cardboard boxes. And you ask yourself: how are they ever going to get away from there? There are not enough hands for all the luggage.

Sarah
I feel like a terrible human being. But it's also a relief. And Peter, Ellen and I have been more close-knit of late. I gave her an extra-thick envelope as a farewell gift. Just look at how much she has bought, especially second-hand things! And then there is a lot she has found, I know that because she often came and showed me various items and asked me whether I could come up with a suggestion as to what they could be used for. She has taught Ellen to rummage through garbage cans. She

has an entire shelf of trophies in her room; just as long she confines herself to one shelf.

Ellen
I don't think Mom should have put her arms around Dad and me when we had said goodbye and Miss Maier sat down in the car. It made her look so alone. I'm going to miss her stillness, oh how I'm going to miss her – I felt like running after the car and screaming.

Viv
I wonder if they're just a tiny bit worried about the old girl who has no-one on the family front whatsoever? Can someone please tell me if I've become afraid of living? Hello? Then we're off.

Peter
The telephone rang. It was the nice man from earlier. The bottom spring in his normally so sturdy Land Rover had snapped from the weight! He took it well. He thought I should know. We shared a bit of a laugh about it. Of course, I offered to pay, in some way or other I feel like she can be considered my responsibility until she reaches his house, and this little nuisance did happen en route. But on no account would he hear of it.

Vivienne
I'm fortunate that I am often placed high up. Now I live above Mr Marsh's clinic, a short distance from the house. There's an awful lot of running around throughout the

day and noise from downstairs, but what does it matter, I'm only rarely here during the day. On account of the clinic, in the house it is only Sunday when it actually *is* Sunday, the rest of the neighbourhood seems swaddled in Sunday all week, even though the men go to work, and the children go to school in the morning, and they return home in the afternoon, the stillness pervades the large lawns and, apart from what the gardeners, sanitation workers, plumbers, piano tuners and nannies do, there is a lack of visible activity.

At night I am so tired that I cannot do anything other than immerse my eyes in trees and shrubs. I happened to think of how in the south it was not unusual for the lord of the manor to have two families, the real family in the big house and then a small house on the grounds where the illegitimate light-brown children he'd had with the black nanny lived (with her). The white mistress often turned a blind eye to it, better an arrangement like that than having her husband running in and out of bordellos, from which he might return home with a nasty disease that she also got into the bargain. In addition, it was tradition at the time on large plantations for the owners to have free access to their slaves' nether regions.

'Mrs Maier ...'

'No, *Miss* Maier, and proud of it.'

Mr Marsh

I am reminded of a general setting off to do battle, leading a campaign, when I see her leave with the kids in the morning. Order reigns. And discipline. Even Paul sitting in his buggy appears to have understood that something important is going to happen and there are no grounds for protest. She has Raymond pushing the stroller, and she walks in front, her arms swinging like she's doing drills.

That it is the woman with the ridiculous amount of belongings in a ridiculous chaos of tubs and boxes who comes marching along with my wild sons in a row, I have a hard time understanding. She is a French Jew, and we are allowed to call her Vivienne.

We have had to reinforce the ceiling above the clinic with a steel girder because it started to buckle, and I had nightmares of it collapsing on top of me and the patient I happened to be treating in that moment.

Mrs Marsh

Today I bumped into Vivienne at the supermarket, where she was walking around with a tape recorder trying to get people to comment on Watergate. She also approached me but I was totally confused. 'But you must have an opinion about it,' she kept saying. 'Make a statement.' People looked at one another and definitely regarded her as somewhat peculiar.

Vivienne

This is my nest, this is my safe place, though I may soon have problems getting in here. Mr Marsh has reinforced the ceiling without complaint – he would hardly want me landing on the lap of his patient while he stands poking and prodding in the mouth of the person in question. (Even though at long last there would be a little of Mary Poppins about me, but she probably floats rather than crashes.)

I cut across the lawn from the main house, which in truth could be called a home, to the smaller house with the clinic and my nest on the first floor. But being surrounded by gleaming Cuban mahogany and Chinese objects with spouts and handles does not make a person less scared in idle moments. Mrs Marsh in any case cannot sit still.

I prefer this arrangement over a room in the main house. The walk across the lawn marks a space, a new chapter, a page turned, between the order and prosperity and that which is mine. All the same, today I wrote my name on a piece of cardboard and put it on the silver platter, against the silver edge, I let it rest there for a moment and dreamed of having a tray brought to my bed, of having coffee from the silver pot. But I no longer sleep in the bed, which is stacked full of papers, so I lie on the floor.

As often as not, someone loses a shoe or throws it away, what do I know. Today I photographed such a shoe, a single woman's, on the path down to the station. I imagined violence, that the woman had been on a wild flight from a pursuer and had lost her shoe. Only when I had it in the box, did I consider the shoe's singleness like my own, but that was silly, because the shoe's singleness presupposes an identical one somewhere else, for example still on the foot racing off at breakneck speed, whereas my own singleness does not.

Narrator

I sit with a magnifying glass pressed against a copy of a page of the *Boston Globe* from 23 August 1902 in which, on the occasion of a photo exhibition, there is an interview with the young photographer Jeanne Bertrand. I am in doubt, and so nothing happens. I keep on staring at these blurred century-old letters with my simultaneously short-sighted and long-sighted eyes. Because what does Jeanne Bertrand signify in this context? She signifies (indirectly) a great deal, because she was Vivian's friend and mentor. And I am captivated by the Saturday in 1902 where the writer met her on the occasion of a photo exhibition... so... I can't stop... jet-black hair... it is too enticing (a pathetic feeling, because it is not a thought, raising its ugly head: that people who lived a century ago were not as *human* as humans today – it can surprise me when during film recordings or in writing they put forward or express something *human* that I am able to recognize; it must correspond to humans who can't identify with people who have a skin colour different from their own and can outright reach that point in their mind where these people don't feel suffering or happiness in the same way as they themselves do). I was surprised when, in a recording from the turn of the century of a ship filled with immigrants steering towards New York I saw a man, who, alongside all the others who were pressed against the railing waving small American flags, lifts his baby in the air and grabs its hand and waves it at the Statue of Liberty – that scene could have been from today.

Now I'm on a roll: photographs of people, in particular those within the tradition of realism, used to dishearten me. Now I have looked at so many photographs in the last few years that it no longer has an effect on me. That disheartenment was the whole reason I threw myself upon photographs and into this book. I thought: it cannot simply be because of that familiar sense of 'that-has-been', the experience of finitude as it's called, that photographs make us aware that we are going to die. Couldn't it (also) be down to something else? Let me interject that I never personally take photographs, I have no desire for it. When I remember something or imagine something, I see it in motion.

What did I conclude? That in all probability it is down to the belief, and this only applies to certain movements within the tradition of realism, that a person's nature or character or simply their mood or state of mind can be revealed at a particular moment. But I am outside of that person, just as if I had met them in reality, and know nothing about what is taking place on the inside. I can't do that until they speak: language reveals everything, *le style c'est l'homme*, it is said; the statement may be hollow, but people's nature becomes clear through the way they speak and write. Because what else is there other than the questions *Who are you? What kind of mood are you in?* that this kind of photography invites you to ask...?

(God knows what has now been revealed about me, that I am more short-sighted than far-sighted, spiritually speaking? For once I sit at my desk. I normally sit in my bed to work, I have a large bed, there is room for lots of books, and for my dog, which is an English Bulldog, according to Maier the most masculine of dogs, it knows very well it is not allowed on the bed. It comes sneaking into the bedroom, but its wheezing breath gives it away and it doesn't realize it. It has been hearing that for its entire life and doesn't notice it. It thinks that sneaking is sufficient, that it is completely silent, and a cunning expression blossoms on its toad-face as it places its front paws on the bed and pushes off, panting.)

Anyway, my gaze falls upon André Gide's book, which contains a selection of Montaigne's essays. Here thank God is a sentence that directly contradicts what I said earlier about not being able to recognize people from other times as being human:

> 'Every human carries within them the human condition.'

Vivian Maier took more than 150,000 photographs, the majority of them of people, a great number of close-ups of human faces where there is little background around the face, little context. I don't know exactly where I want to go with this or where I am inadvertently going with it. What are the bases for her choices? Why did she take a picture of that person's face in particular and not that one? Did she go after something that could faintly be called 'interesting faces'? I know that late in life, when she no longer took photographs, she said to one of her neighbours: 'You have an interesting face.' So it seems that was a term she operated with – interesting faces.

But while every face might express a human condition, a photograph cannot grasp the entire human condition, but writing can, and that was Montaigne's project: by writing about himself to get to say 'everything' about humanity. But the more people you photograph, the more conditions you might be able to capture. In the end you have a catalogue of conditions. But what really is a condition? It is easier when you have material to work with, it can appear as gas, liquid or solid material. I am inclined to believe that conditions with humans have to do with moods, for example restlessness, joy, expectation, suffering. In any case my inner life (and also Montaigne's, a good chunk of one essay deals with this) is marked by large and lightning-quick changeability. One second I am insanely happy, the next sunk into the idea of disaster. I'm just saying: obviously a photograph can't capture that, for that to happen a period of time is required, for that, writing (or film) is required. Only something which narrates can get someone to understand the changeability that is life. And that is what, quite simply, once saddened me about photographs: their rigidity.

Vivian Maier was a street photographer, not a portrait photographer or art photographer. She went for faces but also for situations, human interaction, conduct. A man holding his sleeping dog in his arms, the corners of its mouth drooping, his mouth is also turned downwards. Or: many men and boys in the 1950s stand with their hands at their side in a way that you no longer see – they turn their wrists so that the backs of their hands are facing inward at the hips, and their hands point in the air, a little foolishly. Maybe she went after Time, after the '50s, the '60s, the '70s, the '80s. Or she was simply a hoarder: she collected everything she saw.

She could move right up close to women, men and children without them realizing it, and capture them while they were lost in their own thoughts, maybe halfway between two chores, thoughtful and adrift (alone with themselves in a sea of thoughts). She must have sneaked up on them, and reportedly she did not have a discreet appearance – she was both tall and dressed unusually. Other times she asked permission and people struck a pose for her. Trust and friendliness shine in the eyes, in the faces of many of those she photographed (that is those who knew about it, these posed ones) – and anticipation. The photograph was not for them, they didn't even get to see it, their portrait disappeared with a stranger, Maier, off to some unknown place. All the same, they posed. For that moment of intense attention. For the joy of being seen, preserved, surprised, for a moment of joy, of human contact.

Other times people got angry or annoyed. She photographed them all the same.

Sometimes, when I think of myself as a dog whose jaws are locked around its prey – Viv, trapped in my jaws, close to drowning in froth – I remind myself how close *she* got to other people, how she sneaked up on them.

But now we're on to Jeanne Bertrand – into the bargain I am fortunate enough that a journalist from a long-since-yellowed newspaper page directly quotes her in a couple of places. If nothing else, this article creates an impression of an immigrant's life. If nothing else, then Vivian and her mother lived with her for several years, and she was a photographer. They started to photograph together, and for Vivian it became a lifelong pursuit. Jeanne *must* have had great significance for her. And why didn't Vivian do what Jeanne did, and try to make a living as a photographer, or at least make the smallest attempt to do so?

23 August 1902

The Boston Globe

From Factory to High Place As Artist

This is the story of Jeanne J. Bertrand, the factory girl who has become one of the most famous photographers in Connecticut, and who gives promise – for she is only twenty-one years of age – of becoming one of the great artistic photographers of the country.

In the career of this fatherless girl, a foreigner in a strange country, with no friends to give her a start, and with little academic education, there is a certain inspiration for all girls.

Jeanne J. Bertrand has been one of the most enthusiastic delegates to the sixth annual convention of the Photographers' association of New England, which concluded its session last evening in Copley hall. She, with her dark, expressive eyes, her frank, intelligent and girlish face, which is crowned with a wealth of jet black hair, and her little figure, has been welcomed more heartily probably by the other delegates than any other person who was present at the convention.

For she is known by the members of the New England association and the members of the national association as are few others – known for her knowledge and ability, for the girlish frankness and for her enthusiasm for the art to which she says she is wedded.

It was not a case of precocious genius for photography. She had not played with cameras when other girls were playing with dolls. It is just a case of an ambitious girl, who knew absolutely nothing about a camera until some four years ago: a girl who shrank with horror from life in a factory and whose genius was the genius for hard work wherein she could see some future; whose ambition was to play a larger part in the world than she could play in a needle factory, and who made up her mind, if study and perseverance intelligently applied counted for anything in the world's work she would succeed. And she has succeeded in a very large degree.

'This is the works of a little girl named Bertrand down in Torrington, Conn.' said one of the older members of the association to the writer, pointing to about a half dozen excellent character portraits, the evening the exhibit was being hung in Copley Hall. There was work by famous men and women from all over the country, but these examples took high rank among the best.

'How old a girl?' was the natural question.

'About twenty or twenty-one, I should say. She has only been at it a few years, but she has made remarkable progress. She isn't like most girls, though; she is not afraid to soil her fingers with chemicals in the dark room.'

So it was with some brief knowledge of Jeanne J. Bertrand that the writer sought her out and found her just the frank, intelligent, ambitious young woman he had fancied. She told her little story very naturally and with a touch of pride.

'I have been interested in photography about four years,' she said, 'and I become more and more interested in it every day.'

'But you must have had a good instructor?'

Worked in Needle Factory

'Well, Mr Albee, with whom I am associated in Torrington taught me considerable and I have been studying nights and mornings for four years. In that way I have picked up a great deal. Then I have attended the photographic conventions for several years and that has broadened my knowledge considerably.'

'How did you happen to take up photography?'

'You see my people were very poor and I had been working in a needle factory where they made sewing machine needles. Oh, it was horrible – nothing but the four brick walls, and then the bossing!'

She clenched her teeth and hands for a moment as she thought of this part of her young life.

'But,' she continued, 'I had to do something and that was about the only thing there was to do in Torrington. Finally one day about four years ago I came home and told my mother that I would leave the factory on the first of April. I told her that I meant it and I did.'

'Well, girl like, I went to have my photograph taken and as I was coming out of the place the thought came to me that I would like to work in such a place. So I turned around and asked the man if he wanted any help. He said "No," and if he did he would hire experienced help. He didn't want any other kind around. I then said to him: "Isn't there anything I could do around her. I don't care what it is?" He said "No." Then I said to him: "Some day you may have an awful lot of work to do, and if you do send for me, and I will do anything I can." He kind of smiled and said that he would.

'In a few days, to my surprise, he sent for me. He had a big job of machinery to do – that is, photographing machinery, and I helped putting up the prints for a few days. I enjoyed every moment of it. It was all so new to me and so different from the factory, and I must have made myself useful, for at the end of the third day Mr Albee said he could not guarantee me steady work, but he liked the way I took hold, and he would do the best he could by me. Oh, I was so glad that night, and I came back the next day, and I've been there ever since.'

(...)

'You were not a native American, Miss Bertrand?'

'No. I was born in the south of France.'

Then she told of her father's reverses in his native land. He was a road inspector in the employ of the government. He brought his wife and family of four children to America 'to pick up dollars on the streets,' as Jeanne laughingly put it. He was an innocent artisan, who had lived easily among his own kinsmen in his native land, a southern, sunshiny Frenchman who really knew nothing of America. He died two years ago, and his child knows that he died hating everything American.

Tragedy of the Immigrant

He and his little family went through the tragedy which so many millions of immigrants have experienced while undergoing the hardening process in the terrible crucible of American civilization – the annihilation of old ideals and the substitution of a new

> point of view in nearly all things; the utter indifference of people to cherished customs; then the slow, almost deadening realization that dependence on self is the first rung of the American ladder and that after that life is a battle in which only the strong and indifferent win. All the old home sentiments vanish or have to be materially modified in the new environment.
>
> It is all very cruel when a person has passed the age of adaptability and it killed Mr Bertrand as it has killed so many hundreds of thousands. But out of it the young generation springs with a new spirit and Jeanne came to a full realization of her position in life much earlier than do other girls. It was forced on her. She had in her – resistance. She would not be crushed.
>
> She attended the public schools and speaks excellent English, and she shows that she has read much out of the book of life itself, and that she has thought and studied considerably. A photographer's studio is a great place to study life.
>
> But she has the artist in her. One can see that at a glance. All it needed was the opportunity (...), and, she says Mr Albee encourages her in all her desires for study. He, it appears, is a venerable gentleman who has become very deeply interested in Jeanne, and he acts as a sort of guardian toward her, for all her people left Torrington soon after the father's death. She is alone in the world, she says, but every moment of her time is filled up with study and research. 'I want to know all I can by the time I am thirty,' she exclaimed.

Here I close the chest and let the dust settle on the writer and Mr Albee again, but not entirely on Jeanne J. Bertrand as yet. She has left some traces in documents. In 1908, she was still photographing the wealthy people of Boston. In 1909, she was admitted to a mental hospital, exhausted due to overwork (it also sounded like she had a gruelling schedule).

In 1917, she was hospitalized again, this time after 'a violent outburst' (at an annoying customer? at Mr Albee?), and again appeared on the front page of the newspapers: 'Miss Bertrand Insane Again – Artist and sculptress gone deranged in the Conley Inn.'

Her beloved Pietro Cartaino, a sculptor and immigrant from Sicily, who happened to be married, died of the Spanish Influenza in 1918; for a time Jeanne was his apprentice at his studio in NYC and began to make sculptures. The result of that love was a son born out of wedlock, whom she surrendered to a cousin. There was plenty for her to be unhappy and angry about.

We find another trace of her in 1930, when she lived with Viv and her mother in the Bronx; Jeanne is listed as the head of the family. At that point, she worked as a photographer at a portrait studio called Materne in Union City, New Jersey. Just like Maria, Jeanne came from the valley of Champsaur in the French Alps, but from another village.

We are now back to the beginning. Maria has taken Vivian by the hand, has left Charles Maier, has trudged through St Mary's Park with her suitcases and moved in with Jeanne. When I was a child, I wanted to be a conductor. When I saw classical music concerts on TV, my eyes were locked on the conductor, the way he used his baton or his hands and his gaze and sometimes his entire body to make the musicians aware of what he wanted from them, and I thought the music grew out of him. I didn't know there was a score but thought that the music came to be with the help of the conductor's precise hand movements. Music stands and sheet music evaded my attention, or I must have considered them as a kind of decoration. I loved to see the conductor draw, wave, beckon, tempt the music out of the orchestra. I did not become a conductor. I have my characters that

I can point at, make them speak, turn them up and down. Now I point my cane at you, Maria Jaussaud, I am sweating, and my hair is falling into my eyes, but I haven't had a chance to brush it from my forehead, you who have drawn the name Maier from you as if it was a leech that drank your blood or brushed it aside as if it was a caterpillar (which reminds me of my childhood, when our birch tree in the garden suddenly produced a huge amount of caterpillars one year, it was nightmarish – you couldn't pass the tree without them sprinkling down on you. They were yellowish-green with brushes, and how I screamed and brushed them off me, and how they splattered when you accidentally stepped on them! That year I did not walk on the grass barefoot.)

Maria

'The camera creates loneliness, because it crops, because it draws something (the motif) out of its context. It is brutal. It lies. The camera always lies,' Jeanne said that to me this morning before she went to work at Materne Studio, where she slaps people up against white or other backgrounds and *takes* them – so what kind of a context is she talking about? I mean, the customers come of their own free will, it's completely voluntary.

I don't know what it stems from, what I had said to her or asked her about. I thought about myself. How I have stepped out of my context, how brutal it must appear from the outside. Seen through my mother's eyes, my son's eyes, my in-laws' eyes. An entire forest of stabbing eyes. Jeanne's eyes don't stab. She also left her son to the family, her illegitimate son, her *filius naturalis* – it sounds more beautiful. She sat down on my bed and told me that one day until my eyes overflowed.

But oh how straightforward this new context is here in its manlessness (my son would have been out of place here), its Drunkard and Assailant Charles von Maier*lessness*, he tore everything down.

Narrator
The airy somewhat peaceful 'we' here consists of, other than the two women and the girl, a small female dog, Kiki, who sleeps with Maria, 'because pets are grown-ups' teddy bears,' Maria tells Vivian when Vivian wants to have Kiki in her bed.

Maria
One day he comes for a visit, this son, Jeanne's that is, he is pallid and has dark curls. We are alone for a moment, I'm in my bathrobe. This son must be about sixteen. I'm in my bathrobe, I feel like tugging on the belt, just to open it a small crack. I look at his hands – are they strong? Yes. And his shoulders, too. Then Jeanne returns with her groceries, she wants to make Sicilian food in memory of his father. The moment has passed. He speaks loudly and seems very lively, very different from my own tragic silent half rubbed-out son that life has wiped with a mouldy rag.

I have offered my services as a maid in a classified ad in the newspaper, but admit that it is half-hearted, and hope Maman steps in, that she pulls her hands full of jingling money out of the stoves of the affluent...

Narrator

On eBay and other sites I have searched (in vain unfortunately, I could do with a secretary or a course in websurfing) for the issue of *Town & Country* where Eugénie writes about the millionaires' kitchens where she composed her famous French dishes and sent the servants off with them, up to the high-lustre polished dining tables, I'm talking about the kitchens of the Lavanburgs, the Gayles, the Lords, the Dickinsons, the Strausses, the Vanderbilts, the Emersons and the Gibsons.

Maria

...and hold them out to me. Anything can happen. I have not lost heart. Was it written in stone that Maman was going to become a celebrated chef? Hard work, she says. (One could always go looking for a husband.)

When Jeanne came home today, she had a present for me. She gave me a camera, is it because she thinks I am a born liar? No, she thinks I should have something to do other than lie in bed and dream about furs and men who slip their hand inside. There was so much to do outdoors in the country, first the hens had to be let out, then they had to be let in again, there was weeding and berry picking to be done, and geese to be plucked. In filthy NYC there is nothing to do outdoors when you don't have any money.

At the very beginning with Charles and me, the good times lasted at most a few months. All the signs of affection, I welcomed them, sometimes attentively, sometimes distractedly, always as though there was an inexhaustible quantity in store for me.

I prefer film (to photographs), it isn't as solemn, nearer to life, where every moment immediately cancels out the previous one. If time is a sausage or a loaf of bread, then slice it off, click-click-saw-saw. I immediately took a couple of photographs in order to show my good will, and Jeanne developed them for me, and then we stood for a while reflecting on my proud stiff slices.

Jeanne
You couldn't really say that it is a photograph that makes us leave, but Walker Evans' pictures of the Depression gave us a nudge, in particular (for my part) the one with a woman sitting on a doorstep with three practically naked children, the one child's genitals exposed, all decency crushed, completely powerless in the claws of hunger.

Fewer and fewer people, soon only a handful, visit Materne Studio, and nobody has responded to Maria's advert. That's when we decide to turn our backs on the bleak city and sail Home.

Maria
It was not Art that made us leave. It was when the Lepinskis from the fourth floor moved onto the sidewalk. They were only there the first night, then they moved into the tunnel with all the others, I counted thirty-two mattresses leant against the crude wall, it's so dank that the sheets could probably be wrung out. Nobody looks at me when I walk past. We live each in our own world, those who still have a home and those

who no longer do.

No money comes from Maman. She cannot forgive the fact that I've brushed sonny-boy off on his own kin. I write to her: 'Maman, I've visited him. He's better off with them.' But nothing comes of it, no spondulicks from that quarter.

Today I let Kiki stay in St Mary's Park once I had walked her, I walked off while she was busy digging a hole, Mary full of grace please provide her with the bones I am no longer able to. Vivian cried, obviously, when I came home alone, and I don't think it was such a good thing to do either. When Jeanne found out, she got very indignant. So in order to comfort them I said: 'You know how fat the dogs got during the Great Famine in Ireland.' Now Jeanne isn't talking to me. And Vivian has attached the leash to her belt and will only eat from her plate on the floor.

Viv

We're travelling second class, the very poor have been shoved down into the bottom of the ship, they live in a hole, I can look down at them. They sleep helter-skelter next to or on top of their luggage. Jeanne is seasick and only wants to die. But she has to wait until she gets home to France. It is her last trip across the Atlantic, she says. She is going home to die. Mother walks around counting the lifeboats. She cried when the Statue of Liberty was no longer visible, she called it her American mother of stone, you always knew where she was, and she waved a scarf at the great void. Huge rolling Atlantic waves seen through the eye of a porthole, no – I only like the ocean when I see it from land.

The Beauregard farm is situated by the road, with its back round a bend, and all the farmland bulges out in front. There is a constant crackling sound, like that of a fire or knives being sharpened, which in fact comes from the mouths of the sheep. They graze year-round, they graze their way into our stomachs, they graze to end up as blood-stained skins over the stone wall, and their small spotted hooves end on the dunghill. When I went along to help move them from one pasture to the next, I was given a long cane to keep them with the rest of the flock, to be able to reach absconders. How I lashed out! There were not enough absconders for my cane – I never tired of the way the blow to the sheep's bottom recoiled in the cane so I could feel how elastic the flesh was, without even touching it with my hands.

Beauregard. When Mother returned to her childhood home in 1932, it hadn't been properly cleaned in decades and required a multitude of cleaning agents: Aunt Maria Florentine said she had a cleaning obsession, but I don't think so, because I recall Beauregard being very dirty. It had to be clean, otherwise Mother would not be able to endure it. 'How does that look, coming into someone else's home and starting to clean?' Aunt Maria Florentine said as the grease dripped down the walls of the kitchen and a rather pretty mint-green appeared underneath, Mother was sweating like a pig, her hair was dripping wet, and she was red in the face, now on her knees with the scrub brush. I was afraid of this Aunt, whom I didn't know, and swung up onto Mother's back, and rode her while she scoured, with legs that were too long by her side, and she inadvertently splashed water on the tips of my swaying light-blues shoes. Later we had to move into a house in town because Mother kept cleaning long after there was nothing left to clean. We had to move because Monsieur Paramour moved in with Aunt and shouted when he drank, and stuck his fingers between my folds – that happened in the horse stables.

The view from my room at Beauregard: the sheepfold, black ammonia mud, all their grainy shit – but I have never had a room to myself before. At first, I don't know what to do when I'm alone. Well, for example, I could potter about saying the same word so many times that its meaning has incalculable consequences. The word pumpkin sent me to bed with a fever in the end, pumpkin, I can no longer take responsibility for it even though it is my mouth that sends it off. I draw people dangling from the gallows, neither Aunt nor Mother like it. When I draw people without clothes, I immediately tear the drawing into pieces.

1. I, using my skipping rope, whipped the eye of my doll Alma into pieces, the one Aunt Alma gave me on the dock before the ship sailed.
2. I only did it so that I could then comfort Alma.
3. I only comforted Alma after having destroyed her in order to feel the great warm waves break in my chest.

The shit spawns the flies, like the Great Flood, they enter the house. You have to take an extra look around inside the house, on the cold stone floors, because scorpions might have come in from the garden. The heat outside, the cold inside – two very different worlds.

The dogs at Beauregard: there is the setter Minette, a

hunting dog who is brown and cream-coloured. She has spots and sleeps on a chair outside my window and the instant my eyes open, she stands looking in through the window. There is the Airedale terrier Monsieur Lebric. He eats the flies in the kitchen after Mother has sprayed poison. He passes out. We put him in a tub and drag him outside. Seventeen hours later: the doors open, it's Monsieur Lebric who having slept it off, staggering like a drunken man, is back in the kitchen. There is the cat Minnie, the devastating female when catching mice, with very sharp sudden teeth and claws. I don't have much to say about it. One day my mother pops up behind the cleaning agents and says, 'We're having a party for your friends the Animals.' We gathered them on the patio and arranged a meal for them, something with bread balls and drippings. It would have been funnier if Charles had also been there, the mere mention of my brother's name made my mother cry, and so I said it over and over and over until it was a pure white sound, like the sound a bird in the sky might make.

The drawing room at Beauregard so packed with shiny furniture that it was difficult to get around, all you had to do was shine and you had access. I was admitted there when I had done something wrong and was shining with delight, for example when I went into the sheepfold with freshly chalked shoes. There was a piano too. Suddenly there was something to say about the cat. I pulled my stocking off my foot, put it over its head and placed it on the keys. It was wretched. It was noisy. That was it. I would rather have been too good for this world (but I wasn't), it was the greatest praise you could get. But I wasn't. I stood in front of the mirror and turned my lips down and tensed all the muscles until I was shaking everywhere, and the mirror was filled with evil. When Mother doesn't like me, she says I remind her of Father.

The wall around the garden at Beauregard, the wrought iron gate, the two stone lions that guarded the exit, the road outside that dragged itself upwards, my heavy feet.

'All of this will be yours one day,' Aunt said with a hand on my shoulder, and together we looked out over Beauregard's billowing grounds. It wasn't until years later that I looked up and actually noticed the mountains.

I have never seen anyone in the family dance, but by all acounts they have all gone dancing at the town's dance school, and now it is my turn. I resist fiercely but simply end up being pushed out onto the slippery floor. I am assigned a partner. He wants to dance with everyone but me, there is nobody he won't dance with, even Miss Harelip, in order to escape me. That's not true, Aunt says. I am lovely, I am bright, my posture is just not very good, my shoulders are up by my ears, but dancing will change that. Dancing improves your posture. Just snap your chin up and feel your worth. Remember that you are a star, at least in my heaven. Then the boy Philippe and I hold hands, as they tell us to, and go out onto the floor with the other child dancers with skirts that are starched in sugar, and shoes that are polished with spit; dance school on gravel, dance school in tall grass, dance school in fat or melted asphalt, until luckily it becomes dance school in nose bleed, and I am allowed to lie down next to the wall.

I cling to my mother, I never hear the end of it. It gets to the point where they have to tear her dress out of my hands while I scream. Sometimes when I won't let go, she starts to walk, and so I get dragged behind her across the floor or the courtyard or wherever we happen to be.

The house we move into with Jeanne when Aunt Maria Florentine has had enough of Mother is called Renoul – it lies in the centre of town, is light-yellow and has white shutters. Mother would prefer to find a position quickly, possibly in a shop. Jeanne has saved a little and doesn't need to work, I hope it doesn't turn out like when you put a horse out to pasture and its muscles disappear, its figure completely changes until you can hardly recognize it, so haggard and stiff-legged. The farmhand at Beauregard showed me a working horse and a retired horse, and laughed at Aunt's weakness for animals, he would have eaten the old horse although it probably would have been too tough. I miss Beauregard, here in Saint-Bonnet we are strangers even though we have many relatives, a labyrinth full of them; I've got a bicycle now, people call me the Girl with the Bike when I step inside a shop: 'Well here we have the Girl with the Bike', I always have a trail of toddlers after me as I swoosh through the streets. I love the air here. If I'm bored, Jeanne is prepared to teach me some tricks with the photographic apparatus, she wants to teach me everything she knows. A wife died close to Renoul, and Mother used to look after the widower's children. She has stopped that now that Aunt gives us money. I have nice shoes. There have never been so many people who liked me at one time: François, Maryse, Laurence, Philippe. Jeanne goes for long walks with her camera every day, and says she keeps a visual diary, it's become necessary due to her failing memory. She also says it's a way of belonging again, after all the years in America. The apparatus is her way of latching on. The camera feeds, and a picture comes out the other end. She has turned the bathroom into a darkroom, and says I am her apprentice. But I don't like the darkroom, the strong smells – I have a keener sense of smell than others (and smell things others can't), I've always had that ability. She says the photographs are shreds torn from reality.

'Taking a picture,' she says, 'is always an act of violence. But I can live with it, it's not all that bad, is it?'

We are taking the now-dry photographs off the lines. 'It's not all that bad, is it?' she repeats and holds one up in front of my eyes, of Moutet, whose peak I will ascend when I am older, I know I will return, 'because you give it back, in concentrated form,' she says.

I can see that the Moutet I know is clearer in the photograph than in reality. I am taller than Jeanne, she reaches my armpit. I think it's a load of pathetic drivel – nothing is damaged by being photographed.

'It's because we are leaving and saying goodbye to everything,' Mother says. 'It makes her soft-headed.'

Jeanne comes back with us to New York after all. When she managed to rest a little, she realized it was too early to die. But I don't want to go home. She has become an old French lady dressed in black, who sits with the other old ladies with swollen legs and observes life in the town from the benches surrounding the large tree on the square. 'We're still here,' they say, 'for a little while longer.'

'You're full of twaddle,' Mother says and elbows Jeanne in the side.

'Alright alright,' Jeanne says, and starts to tell us about Balzac's vague dread of Daguerreotypes, but Mother has no patience, no interest in what Jeanne has to say, she would rather just mock and laugh and nudge and tickle, that's why I can't remember what she said.

Mother always wants to be the centre of things: yesterday when we sat eating, she purposefully knocked over a glass of water.

Jeanne and I often bump into each other in the small space of the Dark Room, and one day, I am laughing so hard that I am sweating everywhere, because her breasts shoved me (they're so big, right in front of me). It's time to return to New York, because Father has written that Charles is out of the reformatory and needs a mother. Mother wants to try. But Father has managed to convince one of the Jaussauds to send him money, and Mother is furious all the way across the ocean.

Narrator
Maria and Viv and Jeanne travelled home aboard the world's largest and fastest passenger ship: the *SS Normandie*. It didn't last long. It was launched in 1935 and caught fire in 1942 when it was being refitted into a transport ship (witness, if you will, on YouTube, the blaze on the capsized mastodon). Charles stood on the quay and welcomed them, by his side stood son and brother Carl.

Viv
Carl was not wearing a collar, and Father was not holding a leash that was fastened to his neck, but when he delivered him to Mother it was as though that were the case. Eighteen years old. There were a lot of surprises. We learned about all of them right there on the quay. Father had been to Mexico and paid for a divorce, and had signed for Mother, since she wasn't there to do it herself. And then he had got remarried to German Berta.

Nana had found an apartment for us on 421 East 64th St where we were to live together, Mother, Charles and I.

Two rooms with wallpaper smelling of smoke – Mother and I share one, and Charles has the second to himself. He would prefer to be called Carl, he is used to being called that by Grandma and Grandpa, but I divide him, calling him Charles in the room and Carl in the kitchen. He is not allowed to set foot in Mother's room. He says she treats him like a lodger, not a son. (He says the word as though he doesn't believe it himself). He asked one of his friends' mothers to let him live with her, but it didn't work out. He shows me a document from the prison which reads:

> 'Parole rescheduled for August 1938. The inmate would likely have a better chance of making a successful adjustment if placed outside the immediate family circle.'

That's us. Mother and me. But it could also be Father and his German wife, who are the immediate family circle.

Every night he soaks dried apricots in a bowl of water in the hope of spending fewer hours out in the WC in the corridor, 'You should eat prunes instead,' Mother shouts when the neighbour pounds on the door of the WC that is shared by four apartments. He is big-boned like me, we placed our wrists side by side on the kitchen table. 'Brother' oh yes, but it goes quiet when we are alone, because can you relate to an eighteen-year-old brother when you are twelve? We are not good face-to-face, unfortunately. Flowers won't grow on a dunghill – nonsense, they do exactly that: we ought to be friends. 'You ought to be friends, so you have each other

– in the middle of all this,' Grandma said. Nana (who is Grandma's best friend) pays the rent of $19.50, and gives us fifty dollars to live on every month, and then Father calls her a sanctimonious old hag. The reconciliations are worse than the arguments – we all sit around the table together, but they look in different directions. I feel like lying down on the floor. Everything always ends in shouting anyway. Mother is hurting all over, it's impossible to say exactly where, but her heart is beating very fast. Working is ruled out. We eat food straight from the tin, something Charles learned at the reformatory where the families often sent them extra food, which they ate under the duvet. Nana also sent him food from the Vanderbilt residence in Palm Beach, we are proud of her. Charles shows me how 'Vocational School' on one of the palm tree postcards Nana sent him has become 'Vacational School' (she has never perfected her American even though she has been here since she was young, sometimes she spells *wild* with a 'v'), but it was a tough place, not much of a holiday to it. He is six foot two, and I pray to God I do not grow quite so tall. Mother lies in the bed when she doesn't go to the cinema in her tired fur, which she is considering spraying with hairspray because it sheds. One day when I come into the kitchen, the dishcloth is wrapped around the bread – not an embrace I feel like being a part of. When Father falls out with Berta, he comes home to stay with us until he falls out with Mother. I have seen him get washed down the stairs by waves of screaming and shouting. Carl (I call him Carl now, because he prefers that, and you have to use the name people prefer) is angry at Father because he tried to steal the life insurance Grandma had taken out for him, and he says it is Father's fault that Grandpa worked himself to death because he didn't contribute so much as a penny but bet everything at the race track. He still does. Brother shows me the death notices. There are two because they forgot me first time round. They had it corrected the next day, and there I was in the paper as the bereaved, the grandchild. I often sit on the chair in the kitchen. The tap drips. That's life in the reeds. 'Those aren't reeds on the wallpaper, Vivian, they're ears of corn.' When Mother is upset at Carl, I am not allowed to speak to him. She speaks badly of him to the supervisor from prison, calls him an insane junkie. She says he steals. He also talks badly of her, says she is lazy and can't be bothered to clean or do laundry or cook. That's true enough. Nana has given Carl a new guitar so he can play down at the bar at night, he smokes hash cigarettes so that he can hear better, everything becomes Clear, maybe like crystal. I remain in my chair. Mother says that when she enters a room where I am, she can't sense that I'm there, as though I were a thought instead of a body. There are three things Father and I like: dogs, the *New York Times* and the beach. He has two German Pinschers that scare the life out of people when they come bounding over. But they are as good as the day is long. Nana makes French food for the richest people in the country, and sometimes she sends some of the fine food that will last in a package with a lot of twine around it. I love her packages. I remove the twine – and her presence fills the kitchen. Then we stand eating foie gras with teaspoons, and Mother comes in, looking like an Asian troll with curled-up earlobes because she has been lying on them, bringing in the strong smell of sleep. Each apple is wrapped in tissue paper. 'I'm so ill,' she says, and the heart sinks again. If she dies, what will become of me? The tissue paper makes her both bitter and merry. She and Father both lived in the village's largest houses; 'You know Beauregard,' she says, yes, of course I do. And I want to go back. Father's family are butchers. But there is nobility in the blood from some time in the past, hence the *von*. Their house had previously been an evangelical chapel – it had arches in the ceiling. They were something. Then they came to America, and suddenly they were nothing. The only one who has succeeded is Alma, who has married into Park Avenue. And it must be lovely to cook for the Vanderbilts. But even though Nana visits the grand households, she still belongs down in the kitchen. Carl has bought a padlock to keep Mother out of his room when he is not home – she goes looking for tobacco and money.

Mother now wants to turn Carl back over to 'his own', but Father and Berta don't want him, so he has to live with Grandma. The Germans who are interned on Ellis Island don't want African cooks. The Africans aren't to touch their food. Then I hate the Germans even more. I listen to the radio in order to get good at American again. Someone came by from the census office today. Mother wrote on the form that all four of us lived here, but it's only her and me. It made no sense, but she said it looked more respectable. I am almost always in the kitchen now because of the radio and the unbearableness everywhere else, I have Carl's room now, but the illnesses and the fury from Mother's room flow in. In France, she loved me.

Narrator

Berta and Charles (or Charlie as Berta calls him when it's cuddle-time) have had two of Berta's nephews staying with them; one of them got so scared when Charles threatened Berta with a knife that he fled all the way to Germany, a path nobody would normally choose to take, and the other joined the army after Charles emptied his account. 'Two jittery young men,' Charles said. They aren't going to have anyone else staying with them.

Viv
Sometimes Nana is also at Grandma's when I visit, it's peaceful there without Mother. The old ladies warm each other's feet by rubbing them vigorously between their hands; it's an exceptionally cold winter. I heard them say in the kitchen that Carl is twelve years old inside his head. But he earns five hundred dollars a month playing in a band and on the radio and then a little on top by offering tips at the race track. He takes six different types of drugs now. He tries to join the army in order to pull himself together, but they don't want him. Then Pearl Harbour happens, he gets called up, and we send a silent secret thanks to the Japanese. They find out he is a drug addict, and he gets kicked out. He sits with his hands around his head at home with Grandma again and wails: 'I have no control over myself.'

Aunt Maria Florentine is dead. We have lit candles for her. Now Beauregard is resoundingly empty. The German soldiers have long since eaten the sheep and maybe the horses too. Oh, the horses. Oh, Auntie. It makes Grandma think of a poor old woman she knew back home. A widow who lived alone at the edge of the woods, at her advanced age, with only a cat to keep her company. One day she had got help chopping firewood for the winter from some men from the village, and she had nothing other to give them than a hot meal before they had to leave. 'Whatever kind of roast is this?' And imagine, it was the cat she loved so much that she had served, because she had nothing else, and she could not let them leave with nothing. When I am with Carl, I sometimes think about what Mother said that hurt me and which I cannot forget. I can't really sense him in the room, compared to the two grandmothers who have sturdy souls. It's Sunday. We talk about when we think things have been best in our lives. Carl thinks that the time when he lived with Grandma and Grandpa and ran around with the boys on the streets in the Bronx was best. 'Then why did you run away from home so often?' Grandma asks. He continues talking about the boys and about being out in the open. He loves fresh air like me. Once he hitched all the way to California. Nana thinks her best years were those spent in the grand kitchens, when she was a chef and her recipes flourished on the serving platters, but it has had its toll on her – she looks as old as Grandma who is twenty years older. Grandma misses the fatherland, the woods of her homeland, but so many people have been shot between the tree trunks, two world wars, the camps, no, we must try to stop thinking about it. And me, I miss speeding off on my bicycle in Champsaur in the pack of other speedy cyclists, because eventually Philippe, Jean-Claude, Anna and Maryse also got bicycles.

Narrator
She was close to being suffocated at the factory where she worked for god-knows-how-long at some point in the 1940s, her big hands always wanted to get out, Viv and a sewing machine, she might as well have been an umbrella.

Viv
I was locked inside, behind doors with heavy bolts, resigned to be consumed by a lack of light and fresh air, it's already dark when I finish work and, then I drift off to sleep and continue the next day, the next year until saving up enough money to die. But before that you are scrubbed in Life's great tub. Maybe your shoes will fit another pair of feet that can continue walking in them, in my case a man.

Father had his name in the paper for helping Ingrid Bergman past a curious crowd of onlookers standing outside the theatre, where his job is to make sure the air-conditioning works. I could have stood in that throng, Father too, we love celebrities. He should have got Ingrid Bergman's autograph, but to have been so close to her (he can still catch the scent of her perfume if he closes his eyes and really concentrates, but it is difficult to say something rational about scents, he just says 'it smelled of flowers,' 'but which flowers?' I ask), it's worth more than a thousand autographs, I'm not so sure about that. She let him take her by the arm. He helped her into the car. Her skin was pallid, and he felt her ribs through the coat when his elbow momentarily slid down her side. You're never the same after that.

What are we doing on the beach, Father and I, apart from brushing sand off each other? We are throwing large balls around, and the dogs, now wearing muzzles, leap around in the water as though jumping over obstacles! Carl isn't swimming, he's squirming on his striped towel with his femoral bones crossed. There are men lying in the parks in the stairwells on the sidewalks, all of whom could be my brother – weak dependent grubby men. Father stands in the waves holding a bottle of whiskey, rolling his German 'r's. There are things you don't even say to yourself.

He has no memory. I say: tell me about something from your childhood. But nothing happens. Everything I know I've got from Grandma or from Mother who also got it from Grandma.

Something has happened. Nana and Grandma have sent Mother to a boarding house and found a guardian with an enormous bust who has moved in with me, money changed hands, Mother's were filled – otherwise it would never have happened. It's a different life now. We have put up wallpaper: there are blue roosters on the walls of the kitchen. I got someone to take a picture of us together on the beach, the two of us are like Laurel & Hardy – Emilie is short and fat. She has made life good. I am completing my schooling by correspondence now and the apartment is cluttered with books and magazines; we both love *Life*. Then I dream but I hardly dare say it aloud, of a life outdoors, full speed ahead, travelling, in danger, something along the lines of Robert Capa or W. Eugene Smith. I don't want to spend my days in a dusty studio like Jeanne.

Because I am going to remain untouched forever, I don't need to waste time on bagatelles like hair or attire, I am someone who is going to See.

Narrator
Viv was surrounded by women who did well without men and marriage: Eugénie, Jeanne, Maria and Maria

Florentine.

For my part, I would like a lover with a mind like my dog, simple straightforward, so that there aren't two minds, each like a six-lane freeway, uninterrupted rush hour, racing along, while the heads seemingly resting so sweetly side by side on the pillows – I once had a lover, and often the tumult, the loneliness, the weight became so overwhelming that I could not keep still, but pulled my head away from her head, oh if only it had been the gaze of a faithful dog that met mine, when I accidently woke her and she opened her eyes and let me stare into her bottomless blue human wells. She obviously considered it a victory if she could get me to lay my head back on the pillow. 'The way the dead gauge the love of the bereaved according to the adornment on the graves,' a voice inside of me said.

Now then.

It was the good Eugénie who found the guardian, maybe she used her connections on the Gold Coast, Long Island. Her name is Emilie Haugmard.

Viv

Emilie says we are wiping the slate clean. And no sooner has she said that than first Grandma dies and then Nana, within less than a year. The building that is my life breaks in two, and what about me, I become a very small child in the arms of Emilie, where she lets me drown. When I am lively and on my feet again I buy a Brownie using Nana's inheritance. And a subscription to *Popular Photography*. (A young black man rode a bony horse under the elevated railway).

Narrator
Carl and Viv receive their money all at once, but Maria receives hers in small installments – Eugénie knew how things would turn out otherwise.

Viv
I have returned to the scene of death, to dead Aunt Maria Florentine. Once I thought that loneliness meant that I could be allowed to be left in peace, now I know that it means that there is hardly anybody remaining who knows even a tiny bit about me.

Narrator
When the will is read after Aunt Maria Florentine's death, it turns out that Viv is the sole heir to Beauregard. That makes her mother angry and envious for all eternity.

Viv has gone to Champsaur to sell Beauregard. And to move her aunt's body from a communal grave to a burial plot she has bought in Saint-Julien and supplied with a stone. She doesn't want to live in Champsaur, she wants money to travel with, she wants to take photographs around the world, just like Henri Cartier-Bresson. She sells the farm to the neighbour and gets a decent portion of money from it.

This restless family. Like ants. They scurry across the Atlantic over and over again or from state to state in

America, one of them stays, the other one runs off, and next time it's the reverse. I sit (myself to death) in my bed and watch these wild globetrotters (run themselves to death).

Viv
The baker asked: 'Why do you take so many pictures?' 'Have you counted them?' I replied. He had nothing more to say.

A tiny little selection of my masterpieces from Champsaur:

> A black hen tall as a tower, narrow at the top and wide at the bottom, with her chicks, a majestical proud motherguard, peering across the alley, ready to unfurl her wings and sweep up the chicks
>
> Aunt's new grave (I bought the largest stone I could get) with the chalky-white gravestone with the cross shining in competition with the snow-covered Moutet
>
> Sheep (oh-so elastic) behind the shepherd
>
> A trinity of pigs, head by head
>
> Beauregard, a microworld, the high stone walls, a farmhand, a horse unhitched or not yet hitched, the wagon shafts resting on the ground, the carriage practically tipped over, without a horse as it is
>
> Monsieur Paramour, with a wine-dissipated nature, but he clearly remembered how I bit his hand back

then in the stable. He is shameless, with his purple face and open fly

Grand-père

Good day, Monsieur Baille, because I'm certainly not going to say Grand-père, to start with may I be permitted to take your photograph in front of the old barn, thank you for meeting me, Sir, thank you, thank you very much.

We drank red wine with water (for my part little more than coloured water, all the same it tasted acidic) and ate dry bread and a couple of squares of dark chocolate sitting under a tree in the garden, neither of us were fond of talking about ourselves, so we talked about New York City, I tried to ask him what impact the skyscrapers have had on him, whether he thought by any means that they had been able to compensate for the mountains, but his lungs had been devastated by cordite at a munition works, he kept trying to say that word but he could not stop coughing. I also asked about his work at Beauregard, but it was a perilous topic. He emerged from his coughing with a terrified gasp, so I asked whether he would tell me a little about his childhood. Then he showed me on the tabletop, using his fingers as soldiers, he marched the two enemy armies towards each other, and one of them conquered the other, but a single surviving soldier rose from the slain, turned tail and ran as far across the tabletop as his shoulder joint permitted. (It was you, Monsieur Baille, as a youngster, I thought, where the tabletop was not a battlefield, but the Atlantic that you fled across).

Finally I asked him if he wanted to come and see the new stone at Aunt Maria Florentine's grave, that was if he hadn't already seen it? He could ride on the back of the moped, he wouldn't take up much space, but he didn't feel his health would permit it, well then *au revoir* Monsieur Baille, Nicolas, *mon cher grand-père*, the sinner of Beauregard, the seducer, now a wizened old man who sits coughing out his soul beneath a tree.

Narrator
I remember how eight-year-old Vivianne would not say *au revoir* to people she knew she would never see again, it contradicted her desire for truth.

Viv
I had the technician at the photo lab make the best ones into postcards, we get on well with each other.

I have captured all that this landscape is, the mountains that supply it with an air of staging, it is due to its immovability, and then the snow that can cleanse your gaze (here I happen to recall one day I was at work with Nana, in one of her kitchens, and she served me everything they got upstairs, as the courses came out, and between each course she gave me champagne sorbet as a pallet cleanser). I have finished documenting everyone in the village (some with more than one picture).

I aim to ascend Moutet, but my friends from school, of whom a good many are now grown-up married men and women, several with more than one child, are concerned that I – 'a young woman' – ramble alone around in the mountains, and in order to set them at ease I told them that I'm armed. I laugh all the way to the summit.

Narrator
Of the enormous number of photographs, negatives, rolls of undeveloped film that were found, partly after a large part of Vivian's belongings went to auction in 2007 and partly after her death, and of which roughly two thirds (at the time of writing, as they say) have been viewed, only three photographs of her mother have been found from one day in 1951 at the beach in Southampton on Long Island, but it may well be that the final third conceals countless pictures of her... this is a curious task I'm in the midst of... the material that *inspires* my story is in constant development... I feel like a dog that has its nose right up to the rear end of Time, and it's a little cramped up there... so I draw my nose back. And plant both feet in my story. Then I contend that these kinds of things took place.

Viv
My mother's affliction is that she cannot forget. Over and over again she returns to every single calamity, every single injustice she has been met with in her life, and each time with anger and sorrow; the one who has done her the most harm is obviously Father: he is the Great Beast in the Book of Revelation, I am the product of a rape (she tells me that today like she has brought me a gift on our excursion), she wanted to leave him, but he would not let her go: he knocked her down, and out I came, 'I am really sorry to hear that,' I say and go down to the water's edge, but she follows me, because it is just one of countless miseries that were inflicted upon her.

The sun is shining, can't you just hold your tongue, I think. We've been for a swim, the food has been eaten. I used to feel sorry for her. I used to want to atone for all that harm by being Good, by continuing to return to her. And admittedly: for a long time, I could not let go. I hung on to her, the worse she felt, the better I held on.

There is only one way to make her hold her tongue, and that is by giving her undivided attention, so I say: 'Mother, Mother, let me get a picture of you in your new outfit!' We had packed our things and were about to leave, but now she puts them down and poses in front of the sea, when I take a proper look at her, the affection comes pouring in, and along with all the light-blue and yellow (the reeds) it is just far too much, I feel like throwing myself down and shouting to Life, 'I surrender, your terms are too stringent!' And so I instruct her to take off the cap.

I wait until the sailboat behind her is in line with her upper arm – and now she is standing with the cap she has folded into a triangle. How her stomach bulges, my old mother whose life has passed. Now she looks sly and callous.

Then it occurs to me that we could visit the Shinnecock Reservation together, I've been there myself once before, then she can see people who have had more harm done to them and have lost even more than her, their land, their livelihood, their sacred grounds, their future prospects; at night the girls prostitute themselves: white colonizer raping Native American. I regret it as soon as I have suggested it, because she could get it into her head to ask them to dress up in their plumage. But she's not listening at all, now it's about money, and then suddenly she lights up because she has got it into her head that we could find the property where *The Great Gatsby* was filmed, she pushes me and addresses me as 'old sport' like Jay Gatsby always does with Nick Carraway.

'Mother, that's way too far from here,' I say, and then she continues in the same vein, she wants my money, I had promised her my money, she says. No, I say, I've never said that (but I am uncertain, maybe I've once promised it to her, to get some peace). Beauregard was her childhood home, why did *I* inherit Beauregard?

Carl is simply lost.

A daughter's a daughter all her life, but I too want out of here, I refuse to love her any more, and in order for it to be fair I also refuse to love Father any more – go away affection, go away attachment, go away memories.

It is an immense relief, when I walk through the gate to the family home where I work, that it isn't my family, but that I can get a little family life, test the hot porridge at the very edge without burning myself.

Maria

She is alone. I am alone. She could have come along to see a film; when she declined, I thought that she would end up having second thoughts. I know she prefers going to the cinema alone, she has told me that to a greater extent she then feels like a part of what she sees; she finds it distracting to have someone she knows sitting in the seat next to her, it reminds her that she does not belong on the screen but on the cinema seat and has to go back out in her own life, *oh don't finish, don't finish*, that's the kind of thing I could be thinking about the film. But she could have made an exception, just for today.

Narrator
There's a photograph that Viv took of Jeanne at Materne Studio in 1953, where she is looking at a selection of Vivian's masterpieces of Champsaur, well, strictly speaking you can't honestly see what the gentle-looking person with the combed-back white hair is looking at, only that they are negatives. She has adjusted her expression in the way that everybody who knows they're being photographed adjusts their expression, all the desolation that rushes across someone who knows they're alone or believe themselves to be unseen, is consigned to regions deep within the forehead.

Jeanne
Voilà, here you have my public face, and at this moment I am a celebrity, at any rate I once made the headlines, including some I could have done without, *Insane Again*, a pioneer within her field who concentrates on looking at her young friend's works. In a moment I'm going to say something about these works, which really are quite exceptional. This will become an accessible representation of me that someone one day (maybe) will look at, and it will be clear that it's me because I was in all modesty if not famous then at least well-known. Now I know what I'm going to say in a moment about these pictures of the people from Champsaur, the shepherds, the farmers, the small cowled creature who looks like the bellringer of Notre Dame, I'm going to say that the names of these people ought to be written under the photographs, because without names they become representatives of the shepherd profession, the farmer profession, the rural proletariat in the French Alps in the '50s whereas, 'Vivian, that photo you've just taken introduces me,

Jeanne Bertrand, to the world.'

Narrator
Jeanne looks at the landscapes she knows so well and which she knows she is never going to see again: pangs or entire waves of melancholy and longing, and the places drag the long since deceased parents, grandparents along with them – her mother, her father, the whole wretched business of abandoning the homeland in the belief they would be raking in the gold in America, contrary to all the warnings the letters from America had contained stating that things were not like that. Her father thought they wrote that in order to keep him and others away so there was more (gold) for themselves.

Or maybe she feels nothing. Maybe the thought strikes her (why just now?) that the mental illness, the insanity, whatever we're going to call it, was something she crawled into in order to get some peace *from the sorrow of others*, so she pictures a person sitting down in a corner with a blanket over the head.

Jeanne
There really are a lot of sheep. The shepherds with kids in their arms, three rabbits on a balcony tied together with rope around the neck, they have placed their front paws on the edge of the balcony to get a better look (with the look of aggrieved theatregoers), soon they'll end up in the pot. 'You're good at animals, Vivian,' which sounded condescending but wasn't intended that way. And here are the Alpine children in a row with trekking poles and knee breeches, a boy who is practically

all head and unease. Animals and children, you can do with them as you please, move about, lock up, hit, abuse, destroy, eat or abandon.

Should we talk about composition and responsibility? 'To photograph is to focus, and to focus is to exclude.'

Viv nods (and an expression I remember from her mother crosses her face, it is a mixture of impatience and derisiveness, like when Maria poked a finger in my side and teased me about my Sensitivity). Because she knows, she knows, what have I got to contribute? Then I ask about Carl, but she has no idea where he is. Now Clara enters, and Viv takes a picture of her standing by the old photographic apparatus that we have to manoeuvre down into the cellar. I thought that Carl could have helped.

'Vivian, some day someone will say: That's Clara Materne, founder of Materne Studio,' then Viv laughs and utters her usual ah-bah-oui, I don't think I need to be so concerned any longer.

Narrator

In 1959, Vivian Maier travelled round the world and photographed (using her inheritance, the sale of Beauregard, or that money she might have long since spent on cameras, so maybe she was able to afford the journey by putting money aside from her work as a nanny). From her photographs it is evident that in Hong Kong there are Chinese people, in Cairo Egyptians, in India Indians and so on.

The camera made it easier to travel alone, it was really like having someone accompany you. It gave her a project, a purpose.

Stopping in front of people and staring at them wasn't awkward because there was a purpose to it: taking pictures. Nor was it awkward to sit down to dinner, alone, at a restaurant, when the camera was on the tablecloth, next to her, because she could reach for it at any moment.

I wonder if it has a certain soothing effect through the viewfinder to see framed squares of the world?

Viv

It was the great photography exhibition *The Family of Man* at MOMA in '55 with photographs of people from all over the world that made me set off, off to see people, off to see places; the preface to the catalogue stated that photography explains man to man. I didn't understand. Is it an explanation that, all over the world, you can see children being born, weddings being held, water being drunk? Mankind as one big family. Is that not a little sentimental, ten years after the Bomb? Is the intention an attempt to avert worse atrocities to the great family in the future? It is obviously extremely commendable.

Don't get me wrong, the photographs are marvellous, it's the preface and the sentimentality of the project that make me hesitant. (I might not have seen it if Susan Sontag hadn't pointed it out in *On Photography*, writing that *The Family of Man* denies the determining weight of history, calling it sentimental humanism).

Narrator
At the time, she had already spent three years as a nanny in Chicago with a family of three boys. And before that she had worked as a housemaid in Southhampton on Long Island and various places in New York City. Witness accounts from the many families she worked for are very similar, so I decided to only tell of (and that is to invent) her stay with one of them, namely the Rices (a name made up by me) in Wilmette, Chicago, otherwise there would presumably be a lot of repetition, and nobody enjoys that. I could have chosen the family with the three boys from Highland Park, Chicago, where she stayed for the longest time, and who kept a bit of an eye on her for the rest of her life and helped her when she got old, found her an apartment, sat at her deathbed and scattered her ashes at one of her favourite places, in a wood somewhere with wild strawberries. But to tell the truth, it seemed overwhelming to me to have to manage three children, so that's why I chose a family with just one, being an only child myself I stuck to a structure I know, there are already enough characters to make several soups here.

Vivian made a detour to Champsaur before she sailed back to America. She never returned there, maybe because the money her father borrowed in the '30s and had never paid back had upset the relationship with the Jaussauds.

I'm really not fond of documentaries with dramatized scenes, i.e. a fact is related and some actors subsequently perform a scene that illustrates what the narrator has just related. In dark moments I think that I may have strayed into this horrible genre.

Marcel Jaussaud
Here comes my relative, arriving in a cloud of dust and din, the cows stick their tails in the air and run. In a moment, she will come to a stop in front of our door. She has nothing better to do than race around on the roads. She was a shy child who hid behind her mother or pulled her dress over her head if Maria was not in the immediate vicinity when you arrived. Now she does nothing but draw attention to herself, today she has three cameras around her neck again, how do you do, Vivian, no I don't want you taking photographs of me, and the moped frightens the cows. Do you think your father will ever repay his debt to us? Are you standing here offering me a photographic apparatus? Is the debt supposed to be cancelled then? Do you think we want to be a laughing stock, what would we do with one of those, take pictures of farmers in the fields like you do? We *are* the farmers. You can keep your apparatus, you can put the strap around your neck again. Charles Maier still owes us one hundred francs, that debt can't be cancelled with a camera. I didn't say that. I said nothing when she held it out to me. I just put my hands behind my back and shook my head.

Viv
Does Marcel think that I'm after bucolic scenes, pastorals converted into photographs, idylls?

Narrator
She offered him her Rollei 2.8 C, but afterwards she was pleased that he didn't want it, even though she hardly

uses anything now but her 3.5 F and her Baby Rollei, which in certain moments gives her the impression that it is the core within her from which the rest has grown.

Viv

Mother asked me to bring back the old Rollei that Jeanne gave her, but I end up leaving it behind. Then we would have to sit around talking about photography, something she has never really cared for. It would be agonizing and pointless. What is there to say? It's simply a matter of doing, like walking. Does she intend to sell it? Jeanne is dead, I'm not going to let her sell it.

Once I told her, or rather I aired the possibility that I might become a photographer like Jeanne, then her mouth turned scornful, and she said, 'What do you think you've got to tell the world?' That made me very angry, 'I certainly don't want to end up like you,' I said, 'lying in bed all day.'

Narrator

It's the Rolleiflex Original that Jeanne gave her years ago.

Viv

Yes, it is tempting, but I leave it behind because she doesn't deserve it.

I returned because I longed for stillness but it's unbearable. I come to think of Grandma and her fondness for all the street noise, she couldn't imagine being without it, back then I didn't understand it, and I couldn't sleep because of it when I spent the night in her living room. The noise must have lessened her sense of isolation, it was confirmation that there were other living beings close by. That's where the moped enters the picture: not only is it meant to carry me around, it's also meant to keep my spirits up, we thunder towards the mountains. Outbuildings, extensions, sheds frighten me, all of the things that can happen in them, I think I hear sounds of captives being tortured.

Narrator
So now we've been through childhood, upbringing, youth. Is there anyone Out There who still thinks it's strange that Vivian never told her employers anything about herself? My brother is a drug addict, my father is an extremely violent alcoholic, my mother is bone-idle and sponges off anyone she can get her hands on, none of whom, incidentally, can stand one another.

Viv
People love riddles, the incomplete and the inexplicable are tremendously compelling. I am The Mysterious Lady. The Sawn-in-half Lady, where the past is what is sawn off.

Narrator
That is no longer the case. The past has been glued back on.

Well, now we're back in Chicago, this impoverished piece of scenery erected in my mind by means of maps and Google and Wikipedia and some scraps of poetry – a proper novelist should have been summoned for this project, one of those who, when writing about the Tatars, puts raw meat under the saddle and rides it tender all the way across Siberia.

Anyway, back to Chicago in my mind, probably sometime late in the '70s.

Viv

'Have you ever been married?' he asked. 'No, and I'm still untouched,' I replied. But I change families like other people change socks during these years, I could have added. 'I bring along my life, and my life is in boxes.' 'No problem, we have a large garage,' she said, but still, 200 boxes – that took them by surprise. When they were then done with me and I had to move on again, I rented a couple of storage rooms and had all of it driven out there. It goes without saying that I now have no clue where anything is.

I have stopped developing my photographs entirely, I simply can't keep up any longer. I've come to believe that if my photographs were hung haphazardly on white walls with photographs by Ruth Orkin, Esther Bubley, Helen Levitt, Lizette Model, for example, it's not certain you would be able to say who had taken what. I might not even be able to recognize them myself (if enough time had passed and I'd completely forgotten that I'd taken them). But it's all imaginings.

Narrator

Jeanne Bertrand was friends with Gertrude Vanderbilt Whitney in the time around the First World War. What would it have been like if you had had a friend like that, Viv?

Viv

Yes, obviously there's no way to know that. And *friend* is a strong word.

Narrator
Perhaps if she had drawn you into a so-called 'milieu' you would have been supplied with a circle of artists.

You should have displayed a little more courage. You should have lain your cards on the table. You should have jumped out of the closet: as an artist.

Viv
Ah-bah-oui.

Narrator
Were you afraid of being corrupted? Did you fear your photographs would lose their virginity on the way to the bank?

Viv
I never thought that far ahead.

I would like to say something about my mother. The only time I showed her something I had taken, she said it was *competent*. It infuriated me that she didn't think it was more than just competent. Not that she had any basis whatsoever to appraise it.

Sarah
It's always Mom's fault. Just take Ellen.

Viv
Yes, how is she?

Sarah
She has grown immensely overweight.

Narrator
Vivian! Say the first word you think of when I say: Publicity.

Viv
Eyelid eversion. Where the eyelid is pulled outward with a hook or bare hands so that the entire eye is visible.

Narrator
She is thinking of the dreaded eye examination immigrants were subjected to on Ellis Island to check for symptoms of trachoma.

Viv
Stop making things so complicated. I saw the picture the moment I took it. That was it. That was enough. I seldom dreamed, it would be a lie to say never, of Publicity, of exhibiting.

Narrator
People have compared you to Emily Dickinson.

Viv
Emily rarely left her garden.
I've travelled around the world.
She had a home.
I was continually uprooted.
I'm tall.
She was short, I went to Amherst and saw her bed and white dress.
Her poems breathe under the surface.
My photographs are straightforward.

Narrator
The comparison refers to the size of the surviving body of work and the posthumous publication. She left behind nearly 1,800 poems that were only published after her death. And then the fact that neither of you formed a couple with anyone.

Viv
That's why we got so much done.

Narrator
Would it be wrong to say that by taking so many pictures you drowned one in the next?

Viv
Now that is a strange notion. Yes, that would be a complete mistake.

Narrator
Emily addressed three letters to a Master she apparently longed for, whether it was a man, a muse, God or the Devil. Could I perhaps become your Master, posthumously, where now you lie cozily, scattered over wild strawberries, in the woods where you took your poppets; and while they bounced wildly and laughed and snatched peaches from your pockets, the thought likely did not cross their minds, that one day they would stand there, over your remains.

Viv
You're shameless. The narrator is the real criminal.

Narrator
Dear Viv, you have dragged me across the Sound, on a day with strong winds even, I who almost always sit on my perch and chirp on the windowsill... today, 28 April 2016, I'm standing in Dunkers Kulturhus in Helsingborg, where there's an exhibition of probably about one hundred of your photographs.

Viv
That's not very many.

Narrator
There isn't room for more, Dunkers Kulturhus is simultaneously holding an exhibition on Pettson and Findus. My friend and I, like so many others, are both very fond of your pictures, but they also make us talk about the

fact that we can easily get too much of Realism (we're not thinking of your realism, but of Realism as such) and come to long for 'cranking up the funny handle' as my friend calls the tricks some people do.

Viv
That corresponds to ordering a roast and complaining that it's not caviar.

Narrator
I'm not complaining. I suppose I'm letting myself reflect on how-the-devil you found the energy to take so many photographs when the approach to the subjects, at least those I've seen, seems to be pretty much the same. When it concerns close-ups of people who know you are about to take a picture, it appears that you are looking for that spark of contact it creates between the two of you, and when it concerns people who are unaware, it appears that you are going for a kind of disheartenment in their faces. But obviously there are also all the situations, all the things the people are doing, and the way they look that sometimes unleashes conceptions or stories. Let's take the photograph that could be called 'The Middle-aged in Yellow' or 'Opulent Chickens on tour'.

Two men wearing egg-yolk-yellow shorts, a woman wearing the same coloured skirt, and on top of that the men are wearing lemon-coloured socks. Was it a joint decision the sixty-year-olds made over breakfast that day in 1976: 'Should we throw on our new identical yellow clothes before we go out and look at Chicago?'

Viv
Why aren't you mentioning the composition of my pictures?

Narrator
The content is imposing its will.

Viv
Nowadays, when I'm going to take a picture, it sometimes strikes me that I've been there, I've seen that, I've done that, and then I get so discouraged. Today, a voice inside me said: I've spent enough time looking at mankind. But mankind's garbage packaging stacks, that might be something to delve into.

I have ceased bleeding, I sweat, my heart races, my mood is like a mountain range, first I'm up, then I'm down, I can be nodding off in the armchair, my eyes slip shut, but when I then manage to haul myself into bed, the moment I set my head on the pillow I'm wide awake, with a pounding heart, off across the wide expanses. In the morning, I feel hollow as though someone has been gnawing behind my eyes.

Today I did something I shouldn't have done, I left the children in town, I simply ran off, I couldn't put up with them one moment longer. Clever children, they found a police officer, 'have you run away from your nanny?' they later revealed that the officer had asked, 'no, our nanny has run away from us,' they replied. The police drove them home. I said we had got separated from one another. They knew I was lying. And me, the one who hates lies. Soon I'll switch to looking after old people. I managed to get myself a life with shelter and lots of fresh air, oh yes thanks for that.

Today I found out that Mother is dead. It happened a couple of months ago – that's how long it took the authorities to find me – she has long since been put in the ground. She ended her days at a hostel, a really filthy one, with prostitutes and drug dealers, I know it well, and obviously she left behind nothing of value. I can collect her clothes and some personal items if I want, but I don't think I want to. But something good came out of it. On the same occasion, the authorities found their way to Carl, and now I know where he is. It's almost unbelievable. He's at a care home for the mentally ill in New Jersey, I can visit him if I want to, so now I'm considering doing that. I indulge in the luxury of talking out loud to myself, alone, in my room, even though I am afraid that someone is recording it. I don't think I've seen my tape recorder in years. I've promised myself only to think in French when I go outside. If I should forget myself and talk out loud to myself, then I'd rather it be French that comes pouring out. I met Sarah in town, she was on her way to the beach. 'Talk to me,' I said, 'you are my friend.' 'Come with us to the beach, Viv,' she said. There were some young children with her who pulled and tugged at her, 'I really have to go,' she said, and let them drag her away, but I was not going down to sit in all that light even though I would have liked to have heard news of Ellen. Incidentally, I have through another channel found out that Sarah and Peter are divorced.

Sarah

That's right, we're divorced. An entire epidemic of divorces is at work. The last time I was with my ageing girlfriends, as usual they sat talking about men, such energy to expel, I thought, with all the collapsing marriages behind them, one of them finally got so tired of all that talk that she got up and put 'It's Raining Men' on, and the next second all of us old girls stood on the living room floor with our arms in the air screaming: 'Humidity is rising / Barometer's getting low / According to all sources / The street's the place to go / 'Cause tonight for the first time (First time) / Just about half past ten (Half past ten) / For the first time in history / It's gonna start raining men (...) It's raining men, Hallelujah, it's raining men'.

Viv

When is my Father going to fall down from heaven when is my Mother going to shoot up from the earth, I am alone and live in a corner of myself.

I don't think there exists any deeper divide than that between the old and the young. If you are poor, it's possible to become rich, and if you are rich, you can certainly become poor. White and black can cross one another's demarcation lines. You can change sex if you want to. But old and young, then you truly are in your own camp. I can no longer cycle up hills, it made me so angry that I threw down the bicycle and continued on foot, someone younger is welcome to continue riding it.

Martha's sister doesn't like me, she says I'm making Martha into an imitation of myself, it's due to the fact that I bought her a hat and coat at the Salvation Army, since I had to get a little something for myself anyway. They want to put her in a home, it's completely unreasonable, she can do so much. She loves playing pinball, and it's good for the motor skills; they complain about the housework, but have you ever seen dirty dishes up and run. Take off your glasses if you don't want to see dust, old man. So that's that job. He is a TV host, his wife has departed, leaving behind five children, they think I'm their new mother, and they don't like me, they don't appreciate the things I can do, neither my games nor my food, they only see my shortcomings. One day he took some of *my* newspapers – because they were *mine* – that were lying in the garage until I had time for them, and he gave them to the neighbour, who is going to do some painting. I rush over to the neighbour's and scream that they're *mine*. I get them back, but they're crumpled, and there are specks of paint on them. I spend half the night in the garage smoothing them out and cleaning them as best I can.

A thought has been planted inside me and I allow it to grow when I have time. I'm thinking of liberating Carl from the care home, getting a little apartment for the two of us, just a couple of rooms, and then taking charge of his care myself. Like Langley Collyer I'll go out foraging, he'll be waiting by the door when I return from my what-could-be-nightly excursions. 'What have you brought for me?' he'll ask, hardly able to wait till I've put my purse down – he'll already have his hands inside looking for something good. He'll no longer be a drug addict, because I can't have anything to do with that. He'll have been cured years earlier, that's the way it has to be. Or instead, I'll go out at night to buy drugs for him. If he takes off, I'll go out searching for him. Do I suddenly see him between two officers? Where is all that money going to come from? I can barely pay for the apartment. Then I'll cure him of his habit the hard way. He is no longer a drug addict, done. He is in poor health after all the tough years, but I know better than to put him on a diet of oranges, no extremes with us, nice and easy, perfectly normal diet. I live in fear that he is going to die. I can't remember what we used to talk about, if we have ever even talked. Mother? What was there to say about our very own Asiatic troll, we would bow our heads when she entered the kitchen. I still can't grasp that death could stop her. She was like a steam train.

Well, then I've gone to New Jersey.

Narrator
And you really shouldn't have done that.

Vivian
The care home is on a hill, it is a red building with lots of chimneys, I can suddenly remember the postcard of the correctional facility Coxsackie that Carl sent us, it was also a red building but it was situated on an enormous lawn and had a tall chimney (after the camps, chimneys became forever ugly), the inmates made various things, they had to learn a trade while they were re-educated. *Va*cational School, oh Nana and then also oh Grandma because they belonged together. No, I didn't call first. It's always difficult to know what to call Carl, so I hesitate a little by the counter, but okay, Vivian Maier would like to visit Carl Maier. The glasses resting on the

nose, gazing above them, I think she looks like Paula Fox whom I think highly of and whose mother almost sounds worse than mine. A kind face, a good start to a dubious expedition. Take a hike, V Smith.

'Good day, I'm looking for my brother Carl Maier, my name is Vivian Maier.'

Well, so that's that.

'One moment,' and 'He's never had a visitor before, I'll just have to prepare him a little.'

I'm scared, admittedly, and so I quickly eat a piece of chocolate I was supposed to give to Carl, it sets the nerves at rest. You can't outright accuse them of being busy. Maybe he doesn't want to.

Narrator
Then a tall man wearing a sports jacket and a baseball cap came through the revolving door, 'How are you doing?' he shouted straight away, and waved. The lady from the counter led him over to Vivian and suggested they go for a little walk in the park, under the sufficiently cloudy sky, yes, but the air was not cold for the time of year.

Vivian
Carl has become a digitigrade.

'Do you recognize me, Carl?'

'Yes, I do.'

'Would you rather go for a stroll, or should we sit down?'

'Sit. I don't walk very well.'

'Oh no, what's the matter?'

'It's mercury poisoning.'

'Oh, did you swallow a thermometer? No, that was stupid. I know you know Mother is dead, do you also know that Father is dead?'

'No. I've just been here.'

'So tell me, what do you think of Reagan? He's as smooth as Father, isn't he?'

Narrator

Then two residents walked past the bench where they sat. 'Is that your young wife, Carl?' one of them asked, and Vivian laughed.

'It's my little sister,' Carl said.

'Nice to have a good laugh, eh Carl.'

'How are you doing?' Carl asked and stood up, 'should we go back inside?'

'I brought a copy of *Gallop Magazine*.'

'Thanks, that was a good idea,' Carl said and took it and started to walk away.

'I've come all the way from Chicago.'

'Thank you so much.'

'But are you happy here?'

'Yes, I am.'

'Don't you want to talk a little more?'

'Sure.'

'Do you remember the kitchen with the wallpaper with ears of corn that I thought were reeds?'

'No.'

'You called me "Sis" two times, Carl.'

'That's obvious.'

'Because it's shorter than sister?'

'Thank you so much for today.'

'Carl, wait, I'm taking a...'
It was with his back turned.

When Viv has to tear herself away and leave, there is a moment where she almost wishes she was Carl who lives in the same surroundings and is surrounded by the same people, year after year. But maybe it's just because the trip to Chicago lies ahead of her and it feels so long.

Viv
But no sooner had I torn myself away and walked down the hill than the old joy of being able to go anywhere I wanted returned.

Narrator
The two of you were never good when it was just you two, face-to-face. The grandmothers were needed, beams in the rickety house.

Viv
It felt nonetheless as though the last remnant of Purpose had abandoned me when I boarded the bus and started the long journey home. When I finally got off the train, it had grown even worse, Void, Abyss. Somebody shouts 'Kiki.' It's pouring down. 'Why don't you go in the tunnel? You have to get in the tunnel,' I shout. Then I grab the other end of his mattress, and while we lug it along, I recall a picture from years ago in Queens of three children with a baby carriage, where the little girl is struggling to fit an awfully grubby mattress back in the pram.

No sooner had I found him than I got word that he is dead. Exactly one month later. But would I have visited him again? I don't think so. My three good boys have found me an apartment and pay the rent, everyone always fed Mother with money, that's why she gave up and went to bed and only rarely made an attempt to support herself. But I can't find work that includes lodging any more. I have seven locked rooms with my belongings now. I could take them back to my apartment, there was really rather a lot that I wanted to be reunited with, but I expect I'll only be living here temporarily. I don't know why I put my combings in envelopes, but I can't stop, or to put it differently: I can't summon the energy it would require to stop. And who would it bother? I've never had an apartment before, alone, to myself, I seem to see myself from the outside all the time, it's very bothersome, as though I walked around holding a mirror in my hand.

Narrator
Anyone you stare at long enough will seem strange to you.

Viv
I can see in the bathroom mirror that gravity has been doing its job well and is probably nearing its conclusion, it almost looks like I'm dropping myself on the floor. However, my good feet look as good as ever, from what my no-longer quite-so-good eyes can tell from up here. When I absolutely have to bend down – perhaps I've dropped something I positively have to pick up – I see if there is anything else I can do while I'm down there seeing as I've made it that far.

I know I'm talking Jim D. half to death, and he runs away when he sees me. There is nobody else to talk to, so when I open my mouth all the floodgates are opened. He sometimes lets me enter free of charge. I saw that he caught me shoving food in my purse during the reception at the Film Center, but they're just going to throw it out. It got rather wet in there – *only dry things next time, Kiki*. Every time I come home at night and go to let myself in, I think, now I'm going down to join them in the tunnel. New president, new war, hallelujah. My companion the apparatus lies collecting dust. For a long time, it could not find anything to feed on but front pages, signs, graffiti. 'You sex-happy bastard' – wasn't that a good one to go out on!

Then I lost five of the storage rooms because I could no longer pay for them. And what have you done with my things, where can I collect my things? They were sold at auction, that was meant to pay for last year's hire. It's so abhorrent that I can't have anything at all to do with it, all the grubby fingers digging into my life. Even if I could have my things back, I would not take them. Yes, I would sanitize them. But WHERE are all the photographs now? I try to look at it as though a hurricane had blown them to every corner of the world. I try to look at it as an impersonal wasteland. But I picture bodies, with their limbs chopped off.

Narrator
There were uncashed cheques worth thousands of dollars in your boxes. Why didn't you cash them? You're always short of money and borrow small sums from here and there which are difficult for you to repay.

Viv
I saved them for hard times. Those of us who grew up during the Depression learned to always set a little something aside for a rainy day.

Narrator
You collected cheques too, admit it. You couldn't part with them. By the way, there was a canister of teeth in one of the boxes that was sold at auction. Vivian, whose teeth were they?

Viv
They were the children's teeth, that goes without saying. I don't like you.

Narrator
Which children?

Viv
They're mine and Carl's teeth.

Narrator
They don't look like baby teeth.

Her three good boys who are grown men with beards and children have got her an apartment in a better neighbourhood. They also came and helped her clean the old one when she moved out, which is to say Viv sat in a chair with the newspaper and told them where they could find chlorine and ammonia.

She is virtually only there when she sleeps. She sits on a bench most of the day, right down by the lake, all wrapped up, because it's November now. When her neighbours go past, she shouts advice at them, 'Put on a hat so your ears don't freeze off!', or 'Put a bell on your bike, or 'Water your flowers, they're dying!', or 'That skirt could be a little longer.'

She always has a can opener and a spoon with her and eats the food straight from the tin.

'But aren't you going to warm it up?'

'But I like it this way,' and then she thinks of Carl and remembers his despair at having so little self-control.

'You have an interesting face,' she says, and makes room on the bench for the man with the interesting face. He carries a wind instrument with him and blows notes out across the lake. One of the leafless trees is full of pigeons; a magpie is perched at the very top and the sun strikes its white breast.

Viv

When Obama is elected and I am standing in Grant Park sending jubilant cries towards the heavens, along with many others, I am even happier than when Kennedy was elected, or at least equally happy – I almost wish I had dusted off the old apparatus. Everyone is taking photos, completely at random, with their cell phones, just holding them in the air and shooting with no moderation.

A young girl embraces everyone she sees, me as well, I let it happen (it doesn't disgust me), those were some splendid arms, but my bones cracked like a bird.

Narrator

It would be symmetrically pleasing (in so far as we're almost ending where we started) to narrate that what she is thinking of on the day that she falls – when she gets up from the bench, slips and thumps her head on the flagstones – is the photograph of the horse lying on the street, with its head in a pool of its own blood.

Viv

The ground rose precipitously towards me, and I reached out but could not get a hold. Afterwards, when they had called for the ambulance, I hung on to the bench, but they detached my hands, and I thought about the hem of my mother's dress, how tightly I held on to it, but how in the end they always managed to free her from me.

Credits

Origins of quotations used, in order of appearance.

'A Bee his burnished Carriage', *The Single Hound: Poems of a Lifetime*, Emily Dickinson, 1945.

'Child of the Romans', *Chicago Poems*, Carl Sandburg, 1916.

The Jungle, Upton Sinclair, 1906.

'Chicago', *Whittier's Poems Complete*, John Greenleaf Whittier, 1874.

Aspects of the Novel, E.M. Forster, 1927.

Newspaper article from *The Boston Globe*, 23 August 1902

Co-funded by the Creative Europe Programme of the European Union. The European Commission support for the production of this publication does not constitute an endorsement of the contents which reflects the views only of the authors, and the Commission cannot be held responsible for any use which may be made of the information contained therein.

Fitzcarraldo Editions
8-12 Creekside
London, SE8 3DX
United Kingdom

This second edition published in Great Britain
by Fitzcarraldo Editions in 2021

ISBN 978-1-910695-61-6

Design by Ray O'Meara
Typeset in Fitzcarraldo
Printed and bound by TJ Books

fitzcarraldoeditions.com

DANISH ARTS FOUNDATION

This book is supported by a translation grant from the Danish Arts Foundation

Fitzcarraldo Editions